JEAN DU JARDIN

Paperback: 978-1-969919-29-9
eBook: 978-1-969919-30-5
Library of Congress Control Number: 2025922450

This is a work of fiction.

Ordering Information:

Prime Seven Media
518 Landmann St.
Tomah City, WI 54660

Printed in the United States of America

TABLE OF CONTENTS

Jean (John) was born in 1951, (French ancestry) in Carstairs Junction, a small village in Lanarkshire, Scotland, and only started writing at the age of sixty. At this point he was told he had ME (post viral fatigue), so he had to spend a lot of time resting, this did not suit him, as he led a very active life, scuba diving, climbing mountains, singing, acting, and stage manager in amateur dramatics. He was also a Scout leader for twenty-eight years. He spent the last fourteen years of his working life as a driving instructor. He has three children, five grandchildren and retired in 2017 after working for fifty years.

Dedicated to my Granddaughter
Christina Martha Briggs
Yes, Unicorns are real.

I care.

Do you still dare to care.
When others just stand and stare.
Do you to feed those in need.
While others just feed their greed.

Do you do what you can.
Regardless of others selfish plan.
Do you make time to help.
Though others call you a whelp.

Do you share what you have.
Rather than see people starve.
Do you make time to give.
Though others call you a slave.

Do you care who needs your empathy.
When all others do is give pity.
Do you care about race colour or creed.
Or do you jump in to help those in need.

If only we could all care just little bit more.
And excess wealth was used to feed the poor.
And not just locked behind a safes door.
This would be a better world, I'm sure.

Jean du Jardin - March 2025

What is life?

Just what is life?
Life is good, and life is bad.
Life is happy, and life is sad.
Life is good times.
Sometimes bad times.
Life is living, then life is dying.
Life is laughing, and life is crying.
Life is doing, what needs doing.
Life is knowing, life is dreaming..
Life is sowing, and life is growing,
Life is waking, and life is sleeping.
Life is learning, and sometimes yearning.
Life is finding, and life is losing.
Life is full of crazy paving.
Or a friend saying Hi! By waving.
Life is family, so live life calmly.
Life can be challenging.
And sometimes you need a shove.
But all life needs, is love.

Jean du Jardin - May 2024

PART 1

S'ELF POWER

"Muuuuum, can I get a pet." This was said as only a twelve-year-old girl can.

"Ok Ellette you will be thirteen soon. You can get one as a birthday present?"

"Eh, yeh, Ok"

"What kind of pet would you like, within reason, and not a unicorn?"

"Aw ok, I was going to ask for a crocodile."

"You are kidding Ellette?"

"Me, nope." she said with a smile. "Ok, can we go to the pet shop and see what they have then."

"We can go this weekend."

They visited the local pet shop, which was managed by a Chinese gentleman, Mr Shu Ling. It wasn't a big pet shop but on the other hand it wasn't a small pet shop either, just sort of in the middle. To comply with animal management laws, it was limited as to what animals could be kept on the premises, puppies were not allowed to be kept in cages in the window, which used to happen. Rabbits, hamsters, Guinea pigs and other small fluffy animals, were kept on the premises, as well as fish, and some reptiles were kept in the back of the shop.

Ellette and her mum entered the shop and were approached by Mr Ling.

"Good morning and welcome to my magical world of animals."

"You don't sound Chinese?" Ellette commented.

"Ellette, don't be so rude." Chided her mum.

"You are quite right young miss. I was born not far from here, but both my parents were from China, so I am Chinese, but I have a local accent. So, what can I do for you today?

"It's my birthday soon and I want to get a pet." Ellette said excitedly.

"Are you sure want a pet, or would you prefer to have a companion?" This confused Ellette.

"What's the difference between a pet and a companion?" she asked.

"Good question, you can make a pet of a rock, but it will not be your companion, a companion wants to be with you."

"Is that Chinese philosophy?" she asked.

"No, common sense, who would want a rock as a pet?" then he laughed. "But I have heard of people that actually treat a rock as a pet, and others who take a rock with them as a companion, we all have different tastes, so, the person that thinks they don't know a lot actually knows more that they think they do, and a person who thinks they know a lot, actually know less that they think they do, so does thinking work?"

"It all depends on how you think." added Ellette.

"Excellent, now, Little Elf, what are you looking for?"

"How do you know I am Little Elf?"

"Your mum called you Ellette, which means Little Elf, therefore you are Little Elf, and that would fit in with your Chinese birth sign, you are smart, vigorous, self-assured, honest and very direct, as well as many other traits. You are too old to be twelve and too young to be thirteen, therefore you will be thirteen on your birthday, and you were born in the year of the Dragon, which is also a magical creature, and I have heard that name before, you are in the same class as my daughter, who was also born in the year of the Dragon."

"You are Mei Ling's dad." she said excitedly "she's one of my friends at school. She is one of the few that don't make fun of my name."

"Yes, being different can sometimes create its own challenges, as Mei has found out as well, bullies are sometimes difficult to deal with, it takes belief in yourself to deal with these people."

"Some of the others in the class can be very nasty with their comments. What sign were you born under Mr Ling? I would guess because of your cheekiness you are a Monkey. Am I correct?"

"Ah, very perceptive, yes you are correct. Monkeys are intelligent, optimistic, quick witted, and motivators. Now again what kind of pet are you looking for?"

Her mum gave her that look that says don't you dare ask for a Unicorn.

"I would really like a Unicorn, but I am sure you don't have any in stock."

"Unfortunately, we are all out of Unicorns, but if you want, I can get a pony and glue a horn to its forehead."

"I have never seen a silver pony, and I want a silver Unicorn."

"You two are as crazy as each other." Her mum added.

"Do you mean crazy insane, or that we have a vivid imagination?"

"Probably a bit if both." she replied.

"Thank you for the compliment." Mr Ling replied.

A dog was heard barking outside the shop, the door opened, and a young girl was pulled into the shop by a noisy, boisterous, and disobedient Jack Russell Terrier which made directly towards Ellette. She knelt down, put her hand out and said "Sit" The small dog immediately stopped barking and sat down quietly in front of Ellette, but the tail kept going.

"Ah, Little Elf, I see you have been given a magical gift, an affinity with animals."

"I always knew I was magical."

"But that does not mean you can do magic" her mum chided.

"But I can do magic, I just haven't found out how to do it yet."

"Ah! has Ellette ever done something that you could not explain or understand?" Asked Mr Ling.

"Well, one time as a baby, she was lying on the floor and her favourite toy was just out with her reach, I turned away and when I looked round again she was playing with that toy, I still don't know how she got it, and at her fifth birthday party, she had a toy Unicorn, I did not get it for her, I assumed that one of the other parents at the party had bought it for her."

"I am sure you cannot remember getting your toy as a baby, but how did you get the toy Unicorn on your fifth birthday Ellette?" asked Mr ling.

"I just wanted a silver unicorn with white main and tail. So, I looked for it, and I found exactly what I had been looking for."

"Come on now, you are not saying that she did magic to get these things?" Added her mum.

"I am not suggesting anything, I am just looking at the possibility that things happen that we do not understand, yet."

"Come on Ellette I think it is about time we were leaving."

"But Muuum, you said I could get a pet, and I think that Mr Ling can help me get one that suits me, come on, pleeease mum."

"Oh, all right, but nothing too outrageous."

"You are a very unusual young girl. I think you need a pet that reflects your personality. I have something in the back of the shop that was recently returned by the person that bought it. I think that once you see it you will want to care for it."

"Why did the person return it Mr Ling?" Ellette's mum asked.

"His girlfriend did not want it in the house."

"Is it dangerous?" Ellette asked excitedly.

"No, would you like to see it?" asked Mr Ling.

"Yes please." replied Ellette.

"Not without me being there." her mum said.

"I somehow think that given the animosity against this type of pet that you will not approve."

"That sounds ominous, what is it, a huge spider?" Ellette's mum said with an uncertain laugh.

"A very fine specimen of a red kneed Tarantula actually."

"No way, your dad would have kittens if you took that home."

"Can I have one of those kittens as well then?"

"That was not funny." retorted Ellette's mum.

"I appreciate your concern, but they **are** very good pets, they are low maintenance, easy to feed, and handle, would you like me to go and get her?"

"NO" Ellette's mum exclaimed forcibly.

"But muuum you said that I could choose."

"How much does it cost Mr Ling?" her mum asked, hoping to find an excuse not to get it.

"I said it had been returned, it has already been paid for, so the cost is nothing, and that includes the tank for keeping her in, now you can't get a better deal than that."

"Please mum, at least we can have a look at it." Ellette said imploringly.

"Ok, but no promises."

"Thanks mum." Ellette was jumping up and down.

"Wait here, I'll go and get Henrietta" he went into the back of the shop and returned holding a glass case. "Here she is." he put the case on the counter, slid the top off and brought out the most beautiful spider. That is if you like spiders.

"Wow, she is so cool."

Ellette's mum screamed.

"Mum you'll frighten her. She is gorgeous, can I hold her?"

"Of course you can." Other people in the shop came across to see what was happening, most of them did not get very close though.

Henrietta climbed on to Ellette's hand and reared up on her hind legs.

"She likes you already, most animals are very perceptive and can sense peoples' feelings and emotions, that is what she does when she greets a friend, or when she is annoyed."

"How can you tell the difference?" Ellette asked.

"If she bites you, she is not being friendly, if she does not bite you, she is being friendly, if she was going to bite you, she would have done so already, so, she likes you."

Ellette turned to her mum with big pleading eyes "Please mum, I will keep her in my room, and when I take her out of the case I promise I will keep the door closed, please."

"What is your dad going to say?"

"I will just flash my big, beautiful eyes at him, then he can't say no, after all I am his little pixie."

Spiders at home

"NO WAY." her dad responded to her pleading eyes, with arms folded across his chest.

"But dad, she won't be any trouble, she will stay in my room."

Her dad just stood there tight mouthed and breathing heavily.

Looking up at her dad she responded forcibly with **her** arms folded across her chest. "I am thirteen now and I can be just as stubborn as you can, and **you** said I could choose a pet, and I have chosen."

Stalemate.

"We did promise that she could choose her pet." her mum added tentatively.

"I assumed she would pick a puppy or a kitten or something normal." dad commented.

"Daaaad, when have I ever done anything that is normal? I am just being ME, your little magical pixie, and you have often commented about how different I am from other children." she smiled and flashed her eyes at him.

He sighed.

She held up the case so that he could see Henrietta properly, she immediately reared up on her hind legs.

"I don't think that was a friendly posture, I will take her into my room now, bye."

"Mr Ling also said that he believes Ellette has a way, an affinity with animals, and has offered her a part time job in his shop when she turns fourteen, only a few hours on a Saturday."

Dad was going to say something, then changed his mind, shook his head then went to watch the television.

Exciting stuff

Sometimes time passes so slowly and other times it passes so quickly, the last year felt like an eternity to Ellette. Her fourteenth birthday was approaching, her birthday present, so easy this year, being allowed to work part time for Mr Ling, without pay.

Ellette had been visiting the pet shop regularly anyway, to meet up with Mr Ling and spend time with his daughter, Mei, who had become her closest friend.

The week before her first day working in the shop Mr Ling asked her a question.

"Ellette, Mei says that you draw animals, May I see your drawings?"

"I don't have them with me, but I will bring them along next week. Why do you want you see them?"

"They are very unusual animals." Mei said standing beside Ellette.

"Don't tell me what they are I want to see them for myself. By the way I am training Mei in business management so that she can take over the shop at some time in the future, she is more interested in business than the animals. We have talked about this situation, would you like to be trained as well so that you could help her, she would run the business, and you would look after the animals, I am also hoping that by your sixteenth birthday you will be working here full time."

"Are you kidding," she said excitedly "me helping to run the shop, and look after all the animals, yes please, but what qualifications will I need, what exams will I have to pass, that's going to be a lot of hard work. I wonder what my parents will say to that, when will I start learning."

"Ellette, please calm yourself, slow down," Mr Ling had seen a soft shadowy form grow on the floor at Ellette's feet, just for a second, then it disappeared. He smiled. "Take a deep breath and Let's take one thing at a time, ok?"

"Ok, I am calm now." she said after taking a deep breath.

"How did you feel a few seconds ago when you were all excited?"

"What? I felt all tingly, as if there was electricity in the air, and I was full of power, as if I could do anything."

"Do you know what just happened?" Mr Ling asked

"Yes, you told me I could help Mei run the shop." she replied.

"And what else happened?"

"I am getting confused, have I done something wrong?"

"No, the exact opposite, follow me." He led them through to the back of the shop where the CCTV system was operated from.

"Watch, I will rewind the system to the point where we started talking." then he pressed the pause button.

"What am I supposed to be looking for?" Ellette asked.

"Look at the passageway behind you, and tell me what you see,"

"There's a funny shape there, what is it?"

"What does it look like?"

"A big spidery shape." Ellette said.

"That is so cool." Mei added.

"You told me about a year ago that you could do magic, but you hadn't found out how to do it, do you remember telling me that."

"Yes, that was the first time I came into this shop."

"I believe that we have now found out how you can do your magic."

"Tell me what I did, because I don't know."

"You got over excited, when you do this your body releases more adrenalin, which in turn gives you more energy, which can give you the power to do unusual things."

"Adrenalin, that's what athletes run on when they are exercising, we learned that in biology at school."

"Yes, that is true, but it can also be used in a different way. Adrenalin can be used to focus the power of the brain."

"What?" she exclaimed.

"Humans only use a small percentage of our brain, we are capable of so much more, but we have not yet found the way to use our full brains capability."

"And I can?"

"Some people can."

"Am I one of them?"

"It looks like you are."

"So, what do I do now?"

"Learn to focus that power."

"My mum is going to be so shocked when I show her what her little elf is capable of."

"I think you should keep this to yourself until you have mastered what you can do."

All this time Mie had been standing beside her dad, smiling.

"You have been friends with Mei for some time now, but do you know what she can do?

"No, but she is very confident specially when dealing with bullies, she never seems to get flustered by them."

"That is because she has also found her gift. which is so different than yours, a gift which I have helped her develop, or I should say still helping her to develop. You have the power of the mind and Mie has the power of the body."

"What do you mean by the power of the body? Is she so strong?"

"Strength is relative as you have shown, strength can come I many forms. Try to strike Mie."

"What?"

"Try to hit her, as hard as you want."

"But I don't want to hit her."

"You won't be able to hit me anyway." Mie chided.

"What?"

"Mie is proficient in the art of not being hit."

"Does that mean she can she do martial arts stuff?"

"Yes, but not in the way you think. Go on try to hit her."

Ellette swiped at Mie as if to slap her, she slapped at thin air, Mie was not there, she had moved so quickly.

"How can you do that?"

"Mie has the art of not being where the blow will land, the real martial art is the art of defence, avoiding the blow, or deflecting the power of the blow away from you, not what you see in films and on TV."

"Mr Ling can you teach me to do that?"

"I am afraid I cannot, in the same way that I cannot teach Mie to do what you can do, you each have found your own strengths."

"Shame, being able to do that would be just so Fizzy."

"Fizzy?" Mr Ling looked at Mie as if to say please explain.

"That's what Ellette says now when she means cool dad." Mie added.

"Teenagers, I will never understand them."

First working day

After her fourteenth birthday Ellette had chosen to work in the shop in the afternoon, from one o'clock till four, because she liked to have a long lie on a Saturday morning, as most young people do.

"Ah! Welcome Little Elf, I see you brought your drawings with you, may I see them?"

Ellette was carrying a large brown envelope. She opened the envelope and handed the contents to Mr Ling.

"Beautiful and most unusual, obviously a Tiger."

"Yes, I like Tigers, but I also like rainbows, so I coloured him in rainbow colours, and I call him rainbow."

"Ah, the next one is a beautiful bright silvery blue tarantula."

"Yes, just like Henrietta, but brighter, I call her Hairy Knees."

"The next one is most intriguing, a pure white Gorilla."

"That is snowball, he is my protector."

"Well, that is one animal I would not like to argue with, and the last one is as expected."

"My silver Unicorn, with white main and tail and crystal horn. I'm not sure what to call him yet."

"These are very good drawings, what gave you the idea of drawing them."

"Thank you, I pictured them in my mind and just drew what I imagined."

"Ah, that is why you magicked a large spider last year when you got excited, what you visualise in your mind is what you conjure, we will need to work on your psychic power and mind control so you can bring these creatures to life."

"You think I really could make these things real just using my mind?"

"You have already shown that you have an outstanding ability, all we need to do is get **you** to believe you can."

"Fizzy"

"You certainly are a one off Ellette. Your duties will consist of cleaning up any mess, and restocking he shelves, and to help our customers find what they are looking for, if a customer asks you a question you do not know the answer to, then come and get me, OK."

"Ok, where is Mei, Mr Ling?"

"She is in the back of the shop checking on the stock we have, to see what we need to order. Do you want you go and say hello?"

"Yes please."

"Off you go then."

First step to 'Self Power

During her working day Ellette was normally kept very busy, so at four o'clock each Saturday before she went home Mr Ling would take her through to the back of the shop to work on her powers. She would sit on a mat on the floor legs in the lotus position and hands on her knees. Mr Ling encouraged her to visualise her animal drawings in mind and will them to come to life. For quite a while nothing happened.

"We need you to find a reason to bring them to life. Keep your eyes closed, now you are out for a walk in the woods, the ground under you gives way and you fall into a deep well. You are not badly hurt but you can't climb out yourself, you start to panic. How do you get out of the well, which of your animal friends could be the best help to you?"

"Not Hairy Knees, but Rainbow could climb the walls with his sharp claws."

"Because you are panicking, can you feel the electricity tingling in your body?

"Yes I can."

"That tingling is adrenalin building which will give you power. Look for the energy that is in the air around you. If you are in a situation where others want to harm you, you can feed off their energy, you can use their energy against them. Now call for Rainbow to come and help you."

"Come, Rainbow" she said quietly.

"Now with the vision of Rainbow in your mind, keep that focus and say it louder, and keep building the volume of your voice."

"Rainbow, **Rainbow, Rainbow, Rainbow, Rainbow**"

"Now open your eyes."

Ellette opened her eyes and there in front of her was a small rainbow coloured tiger about the size of a kitten.

"Wow! He is gorgeous, but why is he so small?"

"You are young yet, as you get older you will become more powerful and so will your animals."

"Is he real?"

"Only one way to find out, pick him up if you can."

She tentatively reached out for the small rainbow kitten, which mewed softly and jumped into her open hand.

"He is so soft." she said as she started to cuddle him.

"Well done that is a big step forward, now you know what to do we will build on that small start, now send him back."

"I don't want to send him back I just want to sit and cuddle him. Can I show him to Mei?"

"You don't have to she has been standing behind you all the time."

Mei was just as excited as Ellette was, she started to jump up and down clapping her hands. Ellette held Rainbow up to Mei, he started to hiss at her.

"Remember these are your animals and only respond to you, they will need to be trained to accept others as your friends, I think you should send him back now."

"How do I do that?" she asked.

"How do you think?"

"Home" she said softly, and rainbow started to dissolve in her hands.

Her training continued over the next months, she also started practising in her bedroom. As she got more confident in her abilities her animal friends became larger and easier to call.

Unwanted visitors

It had to happen at some point, Ellette had been working in the shop for almost a year without any real problems. She saw this problem coming even before the door opened, the school bully and his pals were walking towards the door with their eyes turned towards the inside of the shop, evil sneers on their faces. Mr Ling was in the back of the shop, so it was only Ellette and Mei that were there to deal with customers. The door opened and the head bully walked in on his own. The others were standing outside laughing. He was in the year above them at school, and a head taller that Ellette and Mei, he lived to push the smaller and younger people around. The whole school was frightened of him. He liked to be called Slugger.

"Hi Fish Face" he said to Mei, he knew that Ling was also a type of fish. Mei just ignored him.

"Don't you dare ignore me, Fish Face." he said as he walked towards Mei. Ellette moved so that she stood in front of him. She was looking up at him with loathing on her face, and a thought in her mind. Hairy Knees.

"Out of my way, shrimp." He put his hand out to push her away.

"Don't you dare put your hand om me." she said as forcibly as she could. He just laughed at her.

Ellette could feel the electrical tingle start in her hands and build up till her whole body was full of energy.

"HAIRY KNEES" she shouted up into his face.

He burst out laughing.

"Why are you calling me that? I don't have hairy knees."

"I know **you** don't, but I do."

A translucent blue cloud appeared behind him; this cloud started to grow and firm up. A spider shape appeared in the mist; it almost filled the floor space between the shelves.

Mei started giggling, she has seen Hairy Knees before but never as big and vibrant as she was now.

"What are you laughing at Fishface" he sneered at Mei.

"Why don't you look behind you and find out, Slugger" She taunted and then smiled.

By this time Hairy Knees was standing up on her four hind legs and reaching up with her front legs which were now level with the bully's head. One of her legs touched his shoulder; to accompany the touch she started to work her mandibles, which sounded like chopstick clicking together.

"Are you trying to frighten me, shrimp? You have no chance in doing that."

"It's not us that will frighten you it's what is standing behind you, why don't you turn round and see what it is?" Ellette said softly.

"Nothing frightens me, I am scared of nothing." He retorted.

"Well, there is no reason not to turn round then, is there?" Mei chided.

He turned round quickly, and came face to face with Hairy Knees, then he fell backwards onto his backside on the floor in front of Ellette. His mouth opened but no sound came out.

"So, not frightened are we?" Ellette taunted.

He scrambled backwards as fast as he could. but Hairy Knees kept pace with him. He finally gave in to his fear, screamed, then ran for the door, shouting 'big blue spider' over and over again. Ellette and Mei were laughing so hard. He ran past his pals who were all looking at him in total disbelief, how could he be frightened of these two little girls.

His pals came into the shop. Ellette had already called for Hairy Knees to go home.

"What did you do to him, where's the big blue spider?"

Ellette put her hand inside her shop overall, focused, and whispered, 'Hand size Hairy Knees' she pulled her hand out holding a blue tarantula.

"You mean this one?" she said.

"Wow, that's gross!" one of the boys said.

"Do you want to hold her? She won't bite you, well not very hard anyway." Ellette asked.

The boys started to back away, then they turned and ran out of the shop.

"Well done you two, now that was impressive, I don't think you will be bothered by Mr Slugger anymore." Mr Ling was standing in the doorway to the back of the shop.

"If you could see Hairy Knees, why couldn't the others see him?" Ellette asked him.

"They were further away, outside your power zone, and they did not understand what was happening anyway, it was not until they got closer that they could see your spider, and I knew what to look for. Your ability and talent are growing, especially when you are motivated, that was the largest Hairy Knees I have seen you apparate."

"I am sure Mei could have handled them herself, but he was just so annoying. What was that word you used?"

"Apparate, from the Latin word apparatus, just means to make appear." he clarified.

"Mr Ling is there anything that you don't know?" she questioned.

"AH! there are many things I do not know, like how you do what you do" They all laughed.

Decision time

Work at the shop continued as did schoolwork, and time passes so quickly sometimes.

Ellette was approaching her sixteenth birthday, decision time, stay on at school or work full time at the shop? Obviously, her mum and dad wanted her to stay on at school and get more qualifications. Easy question to answer really, she still wanted to learn more, so another year at school was decided on. She would still work part time in the shop. Mie was also going to continue at school to learn more about business management.

As well as her practice at the shop with Mr Ling, Ellette also continued to practise at home in her bedroom, she could bring all her animals to life now without external motivation. Henrietta was a really good pet but sometimes Ellette wanted something more, so she started to bring rainbow to life more often, not full tiger size, just a nice size to cuddle, Labrador dog size. She often fell asleep cuddling him, knowing that as soon as she fell asleep, he would disappear. Her mum and dad still had no idea of her abilities, and on occasion she almost got caught with Rainbow when her mum entered her room unannounced. She had tried to bring her unicorn to life but all she could manage was what she had done as a child, a cuddly toy one, most frustrating.

As she passed her sixteenth birthday, she felt something change within her, she was no longer classed as a child, she saw herself as a young adult, and her outlook became more focused and more mature.

Final step

It was dark, and she was on her way home, the lighting was far from being good enough to light the street. She did not even know there was anybody there until he was standing in front of her, pointing a knife at her face. He had been standing behind a tall hedge waiting for his next victim.

"My you're a small one, I must be about a foot taller than you, but we can have some fun anyway."

She was still small, about one metre fifty-two centimetres tall and petitely built, but what she lacked in size she made up for in personality and strength of will.

She had been told by others not to walk in this area on her own, but stubbornness was one of her other traits.

"Oh, what a big brave man, needing such a big a knife to threaten such a little pixie like me, does holding that make you feel more of a man, do you want to rob me, just frighten me, or something else?"

"You should be scared of me little girl, I can do bad things to you."

"One, I am not a little girl, I am sixteen and a young woman, and two, why should I be frightened of a bully and coward like you?"

"What?" he scoffed.

"And, I also have my protector with me."

"Where is he? I will take care of him as well" he looked around but there was nobody else about. He raised his voice "Where is he?"

"Oh, you can't see him, he only shows himself when I call him."

"Is he hiding somewhere close by?"

"No, he is standing behind you."

He turned around quickly, there was nobody there, he was starting to get annoyed.

"Are you winding me up." he shouted at her.

"NO, but you are starting to annoy me, and I need to get annoyed before I can call for him."

"Well call him then." He shouted into her face.

"I need my protector." she focused her mind and called loudly.

The streetlights started to dim as if energy was being drained from the world itself, and the air felt heavy with latent power.

"Look, nothing is happening." He told her.

Unbeknown to him a white mist started to manifest itself silently behind him, the mist cleared to reveal a two and a half metre tall white Gorilla hunched over with his knuckles on the ground, the Gorilla leaned forward and with a low rumble breathed on the back of the mugger's neck. That got his attention. He turned slowly.

"Now tell him off, Snowball."

The Gorilla took a deep breath then growled so loud (think of the loudest noise you can think of then multiply that by ten, that's how loud it was) right in the man's face, the shock of the noise and facing a creature like that, and as close as that would turn any body's bowels to water, the resulting smell was none too attractive.

"Now. If you want to pick on somebody, pick on somebody your own size, or better still just don't do it at all, you never know what they might be capable of. Have you learned a valuable lesson today" He nodded his head slowly "Good, If I hear of you doing this again I will let Snowball hurt you next time, and I am sure you do not want that?" He nodded then shook his head very slowly "Now go away and be a good little boy." He ran away as fast as his soggy condition would allow.

"Well done, Snowball" she reached up and scratched him under the chin, the Gorilla growled and smiled "you know the mind is such a powerful thing when used properly. I wonder. I have always wanted my Silver Unicorn."

She focused all her power again; adrenaline was still running in excess in her body after her altercation with the potential mugger.

"I want my Unicorn" she shouted. Snowball started to dissipate, and a new shape started to form. A beautiful full-sized silver Unicorn with crystal horn, long snow-white mane and tail was standing before her.

"Wow, you are beautiful, just as I pictured you. Are you a male?"

The unicorn put his head down and poked Ellette in the chest with his Crystal horn, then he reared up on his hind legs.

"Oh, yes you are, and you are real, can I ride on your back?"

He nodded his head as if to say you are the boss, he was horse size, so he knelt down to let her climb on to his back.

She climbed on "I will call you Lightning. Can you take me home please?"

He set off at a tremendous pace.

"You won't let me fall off, will you?" He shook his head gently "My mum is going to get such a shock, FASTER Lightning FASTER."

PART 2

S'Elf Control

Joyous are those that can escape from reality using only their own imagination.

On her way home, after creating Lightning, her silver unicorn, Ellette was having the time of her life. She was sixteen, without a care in the world, working part time in the pet shop, so she had some money in her pocket, and she had her unicorn and other exotic animal friends she could call on at any time.

Lightning was so fast and powerful that he was jumping right over parked cars. Ellette was laughing so hard nothing else seemed to matter, apart from holding on tight to Lightning's mane, but no matter what was happening she knew he would never let her fall off. Other road users were confused about what they had seen, because it looked as though there was a fast-moving silver cloud overtaking them.

All good things must come to an end. Lightning started to slow down as they approached Ellette's house. He slowed to walking pace and squeezed through the garden gate. Although Lightning was a unicorn, he was also the size of a fully grown horse, about sixteen hands at the shoulders. He walked slowly up the garden path, hooves clip clopping on the concrete slabs, he lowered his head and pressed the doorbell button with his sparkling crystal horn, bing bong, they heard the bell sound inside the house. Lightning moved back so that he was side on the front door with his hooves on the grass at each side of the path, Ellette was sitting proudly on his back. The door opened.

"Hi Mum, told you I was magic."

Ellette's mum let out a loud scream, then fainted.

"What is happening here?" Her dad had appeared in the doorway "Ellette what are you doing sitting on that horse?" then he looked down at his wife who was passed out on the top step "What is going on?"

"Daaaad, it's not a horse it's a unicorn" an exasperated Ellette explained "Is mum alright?" She slid off Lighting's back and whispered 'home' lightning vaporised and left Ellette standing alone on the concrete path.

"Can you please explain what that was, and just what has happened?" Ellette's dad asked.

"Dad. Don't you think we should get mum inside first?" Ellette helped her dad lift her semiconscious mum into the room and her eyes went wide.

"Did I see what I thought I saw?" she stammered.

"Yes mum, you saw what you thought you saw, I was sitting on the back of my silver unicorn, but don't worry we're not going to get awkward questions from the neighbours, nobody else could see him, only those that I want to see him can actually see him."

"BUT?"

"Mr Ling was right about my abilities. I have been practising at the pet shop after I finished work."

"What has Mr Ling done to you?" her dad asked.

"He has done nothing to me. He only helped me to focus on what I am capable of."

"How did you get that animal and where is it now?"

"Elf power, I **am** a little elf with power of the mind, I can get things by thinking about them, let me show you" she whispered 'Lightning' and a silver mist appeared which manifested itself into a silver unicorn about the size of a Labrador dog.

"Is it, he, alive? Her dad asked.

Lightning walked proudly over and poked him in the chest with his crystal horn.

"Ouch, that hurt. This is so weird. I knew you were special, but this is just crazy."

"I only achieved my potential after I turned sixteen, but I don't really know how far my powers will finally grow to."

"What else can you do?" her dad asked apprehensively.

Ellette smiled cheekily, then said "I want my protector."

Lightning dissipated into mist which then turned bright shining white and started to grow until it filled the space between the floor and ceiling, then the mist firmed up to reveal

Snowball in all his glory, a two half metres tall brilliant white Gorilla.

Both Ellette's mum and dad tried to jump back out of the way and screamed so loudly. Ellette laughed.

"A man tried to attack me on the way home tonight."

"What have we told you about walking the streets alone anything could have happened to you" her mum scolded.

Ellette made a shy demure pose, her hands clasped in front of her and her shoulders swaying slowly back and forward.

"Why would anybody try to attack a poor little thing like me when I have snowball to protect me, anyway he ran away when he saw Snowball" Ellette walked up to Snowball and gave him a hug. Snowball growled with pleasure.

"Get rid of it, send it away" her dad shouted.

"Ok" Ellette said cheerily "Do you want to see my rainbow-coloured tiger now, or my bright blue giant tarantula?"

"NO" they both screamed. Ellette smiled again as Snowball vanished, now they will have to take my abilities seriously she thought.

"You said it was Elf Power that lets you do these things; how does it work?" her mum asked.

"I'm not really sure, but it seems that I have the ability to create matter from energy, or maybe it's transforming energy into matter, the truth is I can't explain what I do, I just know I can do it. Now I have a question for you two, where was I born, you keep avoiding that part of my start in life?"

"That is not something a girl your age should be talking about."

"MUUUM, I am a sixteen-year-old young woman, I know about these things. I know I was born about nine months after you were married. Please just tell me, I need to know where I came from, well you know what I mean, I need to know why I am so special."

"Fairy Glen" her dad said "It must have been. The place we went on honeymoon had a Fairy Glen nearby. It was so beautiful that we spent a lot of our time walking among the trees."

"Don't you dare say any more" her mum said firmly.

"She needs to know, just before you were about to be born, we went back to the same hotel we went to on our honeymoon. Unfortunately, we got the timing a bit wrong, as we were walking through the Fairy Glen your mum went in to labour."

"Outside among the trees in the Fairy Glen" Ellette said excitedly.

"No, we called an ambulance, but you were born inside the ambulance while it was parked among the trees inside the Fairy Glen."

"But I was still born inside the Fairy Glen, among the Fairies?" Ellette said excitedly.

"We thought that the Fairy Glen was just a tourist attraction, and that Fairies were just a myth. Other people in the hotel told us they had actually seen Fairies in the glen, and because you were born there that they would have visited you as a baby, we did not believe them, as we did not see the Fairies. It seems that we were wrong. We often wondered over the years about that Fairy Glen because you did things that we could not understand."

"Wow, hey that is just such a cool thing, I **am** a magic Fairy Elf type person then. I wonder if there are any more like me."

"For the world's sake I hope not" her mum said quietly.

Ellette rushed to her room and phoned her best friend Mie.

"Hi, you'll never guess what happened. I got my unicorn" She screamed down the phone and Mie screamed back from the other end, then Ellette added quickly. "I was about to get mugged on the way home tonight, by a big guy with a knife, I shouted for my protector and Snowball was there, he was pure white and two and a half meters tall. The guy with the knife soiled himself then he ran away. It was so exciting, that was when I called for my unicorn, he is huge and I called him Lightning, I rode on his back all the way home, he was so fast. My mum fainted when she saw him. And guess what, I am magical I was born in a Fairy Glen, the same fairy glen where my mum and dad were on honeymoon. Well say something then."

"I couldn't say anything because you were talking so quickly, but I always knew you were so special."

They talked together for another hour, finally Ellette said. "See you tomorrow."

The next day was Saturday, Ellette arrived at the shop at nine o'clock, Mie was waiting at the door.

"Show me, I want to see Snowball and Lightning" she grabbed Ellette by the arm and dragged her through the shop and into the storeroom at the back. "Come on quickly, I can't wait."

"Snowball" Ellette called excitedly, Snowball appeared.

"Wow, that's so impressive" She exclaimed "He's so big and cuddly, now show me Lightning."

"Lightning" Ellette said, Snowball faded out, and Lightning was standing there looking magnificent.

Mie screamed "He's beautiful" Lightning lifted his head and shook his mane as if to say, 'of course I am'.

"What is all the noise in here?" Mr Ling came running into the storeroom, stumbled then froze when he saw Lightning.

"I did it, Mr Ling, I did it, I got my Unicorn" Ellette exclaimed excitedly.

"So, I see, I am impressed little elf, your power has grown so much and so quickly."

"Dad you need to see Snowball, Ellette's Gorilla he's gorgeous, go on Ellette bring out Snowball."

Ellette was so excited, electricity was flooding through her body, building up so much power.

"Snowball" she called, and Snowball appeared, standing next to Lightning, it was getting quite cramped in the storeroom, it was not a very big area.

"WOW! I didn't know I could do that, both of them at the same time."

"Ellette" Mr Ling said quietly "there seems to be no barriers to your abilities or your power."

"Now I know I really do have Elf Power" she added.

Ellette and Mie were so alike but also so different. They were the same height and build. Ellette was so fair with soft blonde hair and sharp Elfin features and pale blue liquid eyes, Mie was sallow skinned with jet black hair and Asian facial features with very dark eyes.

After turning sixteen both Ellette and Mie had decided that they would not get the tuition at school that they wanted for their future careers, so they left school at the end of term and signed up to go to the local college. They both chose two subjects to study, Mie chose Business Management and Economics, to help her to eventually run the pet shop business, and Ellette chose Biology to help her with the animals, and Psychology to try and help her understand how her brain worked. As if that would be possible. This would also leave them more time to work in the pet shop.

"I hope you two are doing well with your college studies, if you expect to get paid or for the extra hours you are working, you will need to come up with a strategy to get more income into the business, remember life isn't all play" Mr Ling was trying to get them focused on their future by applying a bit of pressure. Their college courses did not co-inside with each other so there was often only one of them working in the shop at any one time, except at the weekends. When they were both in the shop together, they talked a lot to each other about business ideas, what they were learning at college, clothes, makeup, but most of the time they talked about, boys.

"Mr Ling, Mie and I have been discussing ideas for growing the business turnover, a lot of people get their pet food from supermarkets, just because it's easier, we should diversify by selling basic pet food and higher quality produce, or even get speciality food the customers can only get from our shop, and ask the local vets places if we can advertise in their premises"

"Good idea, but vets also supply pet food."

"Yes, we know that. but we can supply the speciality food, they normally only supply dog and cat food, we can supply the rest."

"Ok, when you have spare time go and visit the vets and see what we can offer them."

"WE, you mean US, go and visit them?" they said together.

"Your idea, you go and do it."

"Ok" Mie said. "I wonder if there are any nice boys working at the vets?" Mr Ling just rolled his eyes.

They went, they got information, and they achieved a growth in income. Life could not get any better they thought.

Ellette's psychology course was going well, and new ideas were forming in her subconscious.

Saturday was normally the busiest time in the shop, but the last half hour before closing time at five o'clock was often very quiet. On one particular Saturday, late in the afternoon, they were standing together just inside the front door watching the people passing.

"Look here comes Justin". He was walking on the far side of the road.

Justin had been one on the bully Mr Sluggers sidekicks. He was just over a year older than Mie and Ellette, and he was tall, solidly built with broad shoulders and wavy blonde hair, he was ruggedly handsome, he was the type of boy that made teenage girls knees turn to jelly.

"Look he's stopped, he's turning to look over at our shop, he's walking across the road, he's approaching the door" Mie was giving a running commentary.

Ellette and Mie grabbed each other, for moral and physical support, and tried to take a step back but they could not move as their knees really had turned to jelly. The door opened and Justin stepped into the shop.

"Hi, I hear you two are being called the terrible twosome."

Two mouths opened but no sound came out.

"*Hiii*" he said with more emphasis "has the spider got your tongue?"

"Hi, eh no, it's just we haven't see you for some time?" Mie managed to say a bit shakily.

"You not with your bully friend Mr Slugger?" Ellette added.

"Him, nah, got rid of him some time ago. I hear you two are doing quite well in this shop, are you selling a lot of big blue spiders then?"

"Only standard size ones, we don't have cages big enough for really big ones" Ellette managed to say without giggling too much. Justin laughed, and the girl's knees shook even more.

"I was just about to go to the café up the road for a quick drink when I saw you standing in the shop, would you like to join me when you are finished here?"

"For a drink?" Mie questioned.

"Soft drink, iced drink, tea or coffee" Justin added.

"Which one of us?" Ellette asked.

"Both of you, if that's all right? I don't know which one of you to choose from. You do drink, don't you?"

The two girls looked at each other, both nodded.

"Yes please" they said in unison, eyes full of excitement.

"Good" he ran his fingers through his wavy blonde hair, then smiled "in about half an hour then, see you shortly" then he turned and left the shop leaving two stunned and confused girls standing there frozen in time.

Something went click in Ellette's subconscious brain, something did not feel right, the psychology of the situation felt wrong, but spending time with a good-looking young man overruled all other thoughts.

"Well, there's an interesting situation" Mr Ling had overheard the conversation. "I pity that poor boy having to deal with those two at the same time. He has no idea what he is getting himself into."

They rushed to get all their chores done as quickly as possible, grabbed their bags and rushed to the door, then stopped.

"We haven't got any make up on and these clothes are not really suitable for a date, but we don't have time to go and get changed, what are we going to do?" Ellette was getting quite worked up about the forthcoming meeting with such a handsome young man.

"May I make a speculation" Mr Ling said, "if he is really interested in who you are then make up and clothes will not matter to him."

"Mr Ling, are you a teenage girl, or a teenage boy?"

"No"

"Then how would you know about these things then."

Mr ling just sighed, turned round and walked back into the storeroom.

"Dad's, they think they know everything" Mie commented "we will just need to go as we are and see what happens."

They linked arms on the short walk to the café, just as two best friends would. Ellette started to get a little concerned, Mie was her best friend, and here they were going to find out which one of them Justin wanted to get more friendly with, or did he have an ulterior motive. Well time would tell.

They opened the door and Justin waved them over, the café was set out like an American style diner, the seats were horseshoe shaped, designed to seat six people, with a table in the centre of the 'U'. Justin moved out to let the girls sit in the back behind the table, then he squeezed in beside Mie. Ellette excused herself and went to the toilet where she made a call from her mobile phone, then she returned to the table all smiles. Mie was already getting very friendly with Justin. She looked up as Ellette returned and smiled, as if to say he chose me. Ellette knew better.

"Well, isn't this cosy, you cuddled up to Mie, and me sitting on my own."

"We were just getting to know each other better" Mie added slightly embarrassed.

"I can always get someone to come and keep you company if you like?" Justin said with a grin.

"Carry on don't mind me, I'll just sit here quietly."

"Drinks?" Justin asked.

Both girls said coke would be fine. Justin left to get the drinks.

"He's trying to make us fall out with each other. Remember Pamela from school" Mie nodded. "I called her from the toilet, Justin and Mr Bully are still best friends. I think we are being set up."

"You're just jealous because Justin likes me more than you."

"This is exactly what they want, they want us to fall out with each other, wait and see what happens when he come back with the drinks."

"Cokes all round, easily done" He then sat down very close to Ellette, and gave her a cheeky smile. "Oops wrong place" as he got up to change seats, he put his hand on her arm.

Mei was not amused. Ellette looked at her and mouthed 'see' then added "I think **we** need to go to the toilet."

They got up and left Justin on his own.

"What are we going to do?" Mie asked.

"Easy, he wants to wind us up, so we'll wind him up. Just follow my lead, when we get back, we will sit on either side of him, let's see how he like that."

They returned to their seat, one on either side of him, and sat very close to him, he looked so confused. Both his hands were on the tabletop. Ellette looked over at Mie, then down at Justin's hands, she reached over and took his hand in hers and Mie did the same with this other hand.

"Come on then which one are you going to choose? Or do you need someone else to make up your mind for you?" Ellette said ever so sweetly.

The two girls were so focused on Justin that they did not see the other person approach until he sat down next to Ellette.

"Hi there shrimps" Mr Slugger said gloatingly. "Welcome to my trap said the fly to the spider."

"Are you still going on about that huge blue spider you say was in the shop, nobody else saw it, we only saw the little one" Justin chided, then he pushed Mie out of her seat, he followed, then guided her back in to sit next to Ellette, he then sat next to her. The girls were jammed in between the two males. Mr Slugger was about the same build as Justin but without the muscle tone, more fat than muscle, and definitely not as good looking.

"Isn't this nice and cosy" he said.

"Bully" Ellette said.

"Now that's not a very nice thing to call anybody" Justin commented.

Ellette looked at him and said "Liar."

"Are you calling me a liar?"

"Yes, because you are a **liar**" she said firmly.

"Feisty, aren't you" Mr Slugger was smiling.

"At least I'm not a **Bully**" she said to him, with a firmer voice emphasising the word bully.

Mie nudged Ellette. Ellette turned to her and mouthed 'shush' Mie whispered, 'what are you playing at?' Ellette replied quietly 'psychological warfare.'

"Go on, tell me you're not a bully" Ellette said accusingly.

"What difference does it make to you whether I'm a bully or not?"

Justin laughed. Ellette turned towards him.

"And you are nothing but a liar, and who would go out with a LIAR, even if he was good looking" She sneered. Which made Mr Slugger laugh.

"What are you laughing at me for?" Justin said forcefully at Mr Slugger "I'm only doing this for you, it's you that's the BULLY, ow! my head hurts" and he started to rub his forehead.

"But it's you that's the **Liar**. Ow! mine hurts too" Mr slugger commented. He also started to rub his forehead.

Ellette sniggered.

"What are you doing to us, ow! This has got to be your doing" Mr Slugger said angrily, the pain in his forehead was starting to bet worse.

"Come on stop this, this is not funny, it's too sore to be funny" Justin commented.

They both took their hands away from their foreheads.

"You've got Liar written on your forehead" said Mr Slugger.

"And you've got Bully written on yours" Added Justin.

They both looked accusingly at Ellette.

"Nothing to do with me, how could I have done that to you? I'm just sitting here quietly minding my own business; you must be doing it to yourselves, because **you know** you are a **Liar** Justin, and you know you are a **Bully**, Mr Slugger."

It was Mie's turn to snigger.

"What are you laughing at shrimp, it's not funny."

"It is from where I am sitting" she commented then laughed.

"You know it does look kinda funny" Justin commented with a hint of laughter in his voice.

Mr Sluggers eyes went wide, his face went red, then he leaned forward and punched Justin in the face.

The owner of the cafe had been watching the tension building and came over quickly.

"Right, you two, get out of here NOW, before I call the police" he grabbed the two of them by the shoulder, pulled them out of their seats and marched them out of the door. Then he returned to the table.

"Are you two girl's all right? Not a good idea to get friendly with those two, they are always causing trouble."

"We're fine thanks, we were swayed by Justin's good looks, but that won't happen again" Mie said.

Ellette was thinking quickly then said slowly "we can take care of our-s-elves" then she smiled.

Ellette and Mie looked at each other, then they burst out laughing.

"OK, you take care now" the café owner walked away ever so slightly confused.

"I was getting a bit scared there, how did you do that to their foreheads?" Mie asked.

"I didn't, I just got them to admit to themselves who they really were, and their own psychology did the rest. Easy really, big egos small brains, easy to wind them up. Sometimes life isn't about magic."

"I'm sorry I doubted you" Mie apologised.

"I think that learning about boys is going to be more difficult than learning about magic" They both laughed.

They finished their drinks then made their way back to the shop, although it was closed, they knew that Mr Ling, Mie's dad, would still be there. Mie knocked on the door, her dad appeared from behind one of the shelves, he smiled at them, walked over and opened the door.

"How did things go?" he asked.

"Don't ask" Mie replied.

"That well? well that's life, you can't always judge by looks alone."

"We are going out the back way; we don't want to meet them again."

"OK, see you later, sayonara."

"Mr Ling, that's Japanese."

"Oh. So, it is" they all laughed.

The back door of the shop led out on to a quiet back alley, with big wheelie bins and rubbish strewn about. As they approached the end of the alley, two silhouettes appeared blocking the exit.

"Why am I not surprised" Mie commented "Mr Stupid and Mr Thick."

"You watch what you are saying, there's nobody here to protect you now" Justin said.

The girls looked at each other and burst out laughing.

"Do you think this is a funny situation" Mr Slugger said angrily through clenched teeth and fists.

"YES" they both said and continued to laugh.

The two males took a step forward, unexpectedly so did the girls, all four were now standing very close to each other. The boys were much taller than the girls, but physical appearance and size are not always the deciding factor in a contest. Mr Slugger, who was standing in front of Mie took a swing at her with his right fist, but Mie's head was not in the same position as it was when the punch was thrown.

"Missed me" she chided "winning isn't always about fighting."

Ellette whispered 'hairy knees' and a small blue spider appeared on Justin's shoulder. Mr Slugger saw it and tried to swipe it away.

"Hey, what are you doing, I thought we were going to get these two instead of fighting each other?"

"There was a blue spider on your shoulder, honest there was, I saw it."

"Idiot" Justin said.

Ellette held out her hand "You mean this one" Hairy Knees was sitting on her hand. He jumped and landed on Justin's chest. He screamed just as Hairy Knees vanished.

"Ellette, this is getting boring, how about we finish this off in style?" Mie commented. Ellette smiled.

"Snowball" she called, then said softly she said "Lightning."

"What are you talking about the weather for, there are no snowballs and no lightning forecast for today" both boys looked up at the sky, so they did not see a huge white gorilla appear behind them, but when they looked down again there was a small silver unicorn standing on the ground between them and the girls.

"What is that? do you think a fluffy toy unicorn is going to save you?" the boys laughed.

But Lightning was starting to grow quite quickly. They took a step back away from the growing unicorn and bumped into something big and hairy, just as Lightning reached his full size, but he wasn't fluffy anymore, his coat was glossy and shining like silver kitchen tin foil, only his coat was much shinier.

Snowball put one of his huge white hands on each their shoulders and growled softly. It was now the boys turn for their knees to shake.

Ellette whispered 'home', and Snowball and Lightning disappeared.

The boys turned and ran away as fast as they could.

"Do you think they'll tell other people about their encounter with a giant white gorilla and a silver unicorn, or that they got beaten by two girls" Ellette said.

"I doubt it" Mie laughed.

"You know sometimes winning is more about applying psychology or martial arts than fighting, but sometimes what you need is a bit of your own *Magic.*"

PART 3

S'ELFS

Joyous are those who can see
things as they really are.

"*D*aaad?"

When your daughter says that word in that manner you just know there will be something awkward or troublesome to follow, seventeen-year-old daughters don't say that word like that, unless they are wanting something. So, without saying anything her dad put down his newspaper and looked questioningly at Ellette.

"Daaad. When are we going on holiday this year?"

"Not sure yet" he responded.

"Have you and mum decided where we are going?"

"Not yet. Why?"

"College will be finished by the middle of June so I will be working full time in the pet shop, and I have to let Mr Ling know when I want my holidays" pause "aaannnddd, I have an idea about where we could go" she added.

He called Ellette's mum, who she came in from the kitchen, taking in the atmosphere very quickly.

"What is it?" she asked, looking at Ellette but talking to her husband.

"Ellette has an idea for our holiday this year, I thought that you would like to be here for the discussion part."

She sat on the arm of the easy chair and folded her arms. "Well?" she asked.

"Well, eh, I was just thinking that we, well I, have never been to that place where I was born. I would like to go and see that Fairy Glen, just to see if it's as beautiful as you say it is."

"And?"

"Well, I have been thinking about what you told me about the Fairies, and, if it was them that gave me my powers, I would like to go and see if I can meet them and say thank you."

"You do know that we never saw any Fairies."

"You told me that you didn't believe in Fairies all those years ago, but surely you must believe in them now because of who I am and what I can do?" Ellette was getting a bit excited, she held out her hand and a tarantula appeared in it.

"Ellette, can you not control your magical urges, I thought your spider Hairy knees was blue?"

"This isn't Hairy knees this is Henrietta."

"But surely Henrietta is in your room, how did she get here?"

"I don't know I just wished for her to be here, and she just appeared."

"Ellette" her mum looked and sounded a bit shocked "when did you learn that you could teleport things?"

"I didn't know I could, it just happened, this is so weird, I thought my powers had peaked when I turned sixteen. I really should go and ask the Fairies about the limits of my powers. Maybe they can help me understand what I am really capable of. Please, can we go to the Fairy Glen, please please please?" she pleaded.

"I think, even if we don't find any Fairies, in order for us to keep our sanity, we will need to go back there" her dad finally agreed "these extra shocks are not good for my blood pressure."

"Daaad? Can Mei come with us, she would be company for me, and if I had company it would stop me annoying you all the time."

As often happens when you are talking to your children you go to say something, then you realise that what you were going to say has no relevance anyway, so there is no point in saying anything.

"Thanks dad, I'll go and let her know, by the way the first week in July would be a good time for a holiday."

It's amazing how loud girl screams are when they are excited, Ellette's was heard clearly all the way from her room.

"I Guess Mei was as excited as Ellette. Just what have we let ourselves in for?" Ellette's mum was shaking her head as she walked back into the kitchen.

Mr Ling stood quietly and watched the two girls bounce around the shop with excitement.

"Where is this Fairy Glen and hotel you are going to?" he asked.

"I have no idea, never thought to ask, but I will find out and let you know" Ellette told him.

"OK, but first of all we have a problem to deal with."

That calmed the girls down, they stood in front of Mr Ling, they were looking a bit worried.

"Problem, what problem?" Mei asked.

"You should know, you placed the order Mei."

"The pet food order?"

"Yes" he replied.

"I thought that I ordered the correct stuff?"

"Yes, you did order the correct stuff, but unfortunately you ordered too much of the correct stuff."

"Is that all, we will just have to sell more then." Mei said smiling.

"Come with me" Mr Ling led them through into the storeroom at the back of the shop.

"Oh! That's a lot of cat and dog food."

"Yes, instead of ordering five kilo bags, you ordered fifteen kilo bags, we now have three times more pet food to get rid of. Any ideas how we are going to do this?"

"Eh, not at the moment, but we'll think of something."

"This is Monday, we will need to get this all sold before the invoice comes in, so I suggest you get your thinking caps on."

Mr ling them left them to contemplate the task ahead of them.

"Mei, how are we going to get this lot sold quickly?"

Mei just stood there quietly thinking of the options available.

Lightbulb moment, Mei's eyes lit up, and she smiled.

"Easily done, there is a street fair this Saturday, we can take a stall and sell the pet food straight to the pet owners, and it will help with marketing our shop as well."

"Hey, you really do have switched on business brain, let's go tell your dad."

They outlined their business plan to him.

"Well done, a problem isn't a problem unless you make it a problem, there is always a solution if you look in the proper place to find it. Some seventeen-year-olds are really quite intelligent. Experience does not always make you any smarter."

"What?" Ellette questioned "You and your riddles really confuse me sometimes."

Mei contacted the organisers of the fair and they were allocated a stall. It was an early morning start to get the pet food up to the stall, the girls weren't very happy about that, but they did it anyway, and Mr Ling helped out. It was decided to discount the pet food because they were selling larger bags, and also to encourage people to buy it. The next problem to be overcome was a more difficult one, most people did not want to carry a fifteenkilo bag of pet food round with them. Some customers said they would return later to pick up the bags of pet food, but they reckoned most of them would not return. A better solution a was required. As that were trying to work out a more satisfactory solution. A familiar figure approached the stall. Their old friend Justin, as handsome as ever but he was looking as bit anxious as he approached.

"Hi, you probably don't even want to talk to me, I can appreciate that after what we did to you, I really just wanted to say that I am so sorry about what happened, and if there us anything I can do to make amends please tell me. by the way slugger and I are no longer friends"

The girls looked at each other, smiled, turned back and smiled at Justin. Sometimes things work out well without fighting, psychology, or magic.

"If you are serious, we do have a small problem that you could help us with" Ellette told him.

"I hope it's not taking your sider for a walk?" he smiled.

Good looking, and a sense of humour, and admits he was wrong, both girls thought at the same time, now if this is the real Justin, then there is hope yet.

"We are selling bags of pet food, but some people are finding them a bit heavy to carry, if we could offer a service of carrying the bags to their cars that would be a big advantage, are you up to the challenge?"

Justin smiled.

"Exercise is what I live for, bring it on."

It wasn't long before Justin's services were called for, and the offer of help to carry the bags to their cars brought in so much more business. Extra business was brought in by dogs themselves, there were boxes of dog treats on the stall, and quite a few of those attending the fair had brought their dogs with them, dogs and treats go together, so dogs often pulled their owners in the direction of the stall. As he walked away carrying a large bad of dog food to a customer's car, the girls realised it was time to evaluate the Justin situation.

"You're the one studying psychology Ellette, do you think this is the genuine Justin, is he putting on an act, or are you influencing his mind" Mie asked.

"Yes I am. Yes I do, no he is not acting, and no I am not."

"This could get complicated, back to the old question again, which one of us?" Mie stated.

"The easy way to deal with this situation would be for the three of us just to be good friends, or would they be a hard thing to achieve?"

"After what happened before, I think that would be the best way forward" Mei agreed.

When Justin returned, he found the girls standing behind the stall with an unusual expression on their faces.

"Have you two been talking about me?" He asked.

"Of course we have, and we really like **this** Justin" Mei told him.

"BUT" he asked.

"We just want to be friends, no complicated relationships."

"That suits me just fine, nice friends are good to have."

"Well, isn't this just so cosy, I thought that I would follow you to see what sort of mess you are making of your life without me" Mr Slugger said as he approached the stall, trailing three of his minions behind him.

"Why don't you just go home and play with your toys, if you want to get to the girls, you will have to go through me first" Justin stood his ground.

"There are four of us you know" Mr Slugger stated.

"Yes, I can count."

The girls come out from behind the stall and stood one on each side of Justin.

"Hey Mr Slugger, do you want us to beat you up, like we did before?" they took a step towards him, and he moved back a step. the three others behind him looked a bit uncertain about what was going on. The girls laughed.

"Hey, you three hiding behind this so-called Mr Slugger, yes it's true we took on these two girls and lost, so have a good think about the situation, before you start anything" Justin advised.

Ellette saw movement of to her right-hand side, looked over and saw Justin, or what looked like his twin brother approaching.

"What? Who?" she stammered, looking from one Justin to the other.

As he approached, the new Justin said, "Hi Justin your mum told me you would be here, you got a problem?"

Mei's jaw dropped, she could not believe what she was seeing, she turned to Ellette and mouthed 'you?' Ellette shook her head.

"Hi Jason, love your timing, wasn't sure when you were going to get here, the one with blonde hair is Ellette, and the one with dark hair is Mei, these are the girls I told you about, they are friends of mine."

"Hi girls, nice to meet you as last, I'm Jason, Justin's cousin, here for a weekend visit, glad to see he is keeping better company now, and this I suppose, is Mr Trouble?"

Justin moved so the girls were standing between Justin and Jason. The girls looked at each other, and both mouthed 'problem solved.'

"Four on four now, oops! Wrong, it seems that your pals have lost heart and are leaving you on your own, bye guys, good decision" Jason called.

Mr Slugger stood there for a second then looked round, he seemed to be at a total loss about what to do next, he seemed to shrink in size, then he turned and slouched away.

"Now Justin, I know you told me about how pretty these two were, but I think you understated there looks, they are both very pretty indeed."

"Have you been talking to Jason about us?" Time for the girl's knees to start shaking again.

"To answer your obvious unasked questions, yes, we are the same age, born on the same day but at different times, our dads were twins, and the gene line has been passed down to the next generation, hence here we are. When we were younger, we spent a lot of time playing together, until I moved further away, we were often taken for twins, we had lots of fun then, people got so confused, any comments?" Jason asked.

"Eh! Nope, you just caught us off guard, you are so alike, it's so weird" Ellette said.

"We're weird? according to the things Justin has said about the two of you, it's you that are weird."

"We're not really weird, we are just different from other girls, in lots of weird and unusual ways, difficult to explain really" Mei tried to explain.

"Blue spiders, huge silver unicorns, what's difficult to explain?" Jason asked.

"Ok! We're weird, especially me, in a most unusual way" Ellette told him.

"Are you going to clarify that statement?" Jason asked.

"Nope, not at the moment, maybe some time in the future, who knows, if you stick around, you may find out" Ellette added.

"Is that an invitation?" Justin asked.

"Could be" Ellette said.

"I thought that we were just going to be good friends?"

"Well things change so quickly sometimes" Mei smiled at Jason or was it Justin? they were wearing similar clothes. This could get tricky.

Mr Ling approached and did a double take on the two boys.

"I, eh, I thought I should come and remind you that the fair is about to end, but I see that you are otherwise distracted, no, don't bother trying to explain, I will just get more confused."

"It's quite simple dad. I'll explain it to you later."

It had been a very successful day in more ways than one. There was not a lot of pet food left to take back to the shop, and with help from the boy's things were cleared away very quickly.

Life as a seventeen-year-old, can be very confusing, with so much more to learn, especially trying to get to know about seventeen, almost eighteen, year old boys. And time was short there was only three weeks till they went on holiday.

Decisions Decisions

Mr Ling was locking up the shop but also keeping an eye on the four teenagers who were standing at the front door.

"Take care." he called to them.

"Don't worry, we'll take care of the girls." Jason said.

"I wasn't talking to the girls, I was talking to you two young men, **you** will need to take care." Mr Ling said with a wry smile.

Ellette caught Mie's eye, 'ok' she mouthed, Mei nodded enthusiastically.

"I don't know about you three." Ellette said "but I am really hungry, anyone fancy a burger, I now where there is a café not far from here?"

"I don't think that would be a good idea" Justin stated.

"You mean you don't want to go for meal with us?" Mie said disappointedly.

"No, not that, yes we do, but I'm sure the café owner would not let me in after what happened the last time we were there."

"We could always have some fun with him, the two of you being so alike, come on let's go have some fun."

"Bye dad won't be too late home" Mie called to him.

Mr Ling looked a bit anxious,

"Don't worry Mr Ling we will look after them, but I am sure they can look after themselves" Jason stated,

Mr Ling smiled and nodded as if to say, 'I know.'

Everything just sort of fell into place as they walked the short distance to the café, Ellette walked beside Justin and Mei walked beside Jason. Smiles all round.

"There is something I need to do, I need to let my mum and dad know I will be late home" Ellette told Justin.

"Best of luck with that" Mei said with concern.

Ellette dialled her home number, after a few rings she heard her mums voice.

"Hi Ellette, are you on your way home?"

"Eh! not yet, we are going to get something to eat before coming home."

"And who is We?" her mum asked.

"Just me and Mie and, Eh, two boys"

"Two boys you just happened to meet, or did you know them already?"

"Well, we knew one of them already and the other one is his cousin, here for a weekend visit."

"And does this boy you know have a name?"

Ellette grimaced, then replied.

"His name is Justin."

"Oh! The same Justin that was with the bully some time ago?"

"Yes mum, but he has changed, he really is a nice person."

"Are you really sure about this, you know what happened last time?"

"I'm sure, he and his cousin helped us out at the fair."

"Ok, if you are sure, and remember you always have your protector, be careful see you later."

The others had been listening to the conversation.

"Thank you" Justin smiled then asked, "who or what is your protector."

Ellette went red in the face, and Mei laughed.

"That's one of the weird things about me, I'm magic."

"Does that mean you can do magic?" Jason asked.

"No. it means that **I am** magic, I'll explain later, maybe."

"Do I know your protector?" Justin asked.

"No, but you have bumped into him before, in the alleyway."

"Girls are just so confusing" Justin said smiling "but I do like a challenge."

"Well, you've definitely got a challenge with Ellette" Mie stated.

They arrived at the Café.

"You two wait outside, Justin and I will go in first, then you two come in a few second behind us, and see what the owner does, ok?"

Justin held the door open, and Ellette entered the café with Justin just behind her. As soon as he entered the owner came right over.

"You are not welcome here, leave now!" then he pointed to the door just as Mie and Jason entered.

"What?" he needed time to think "I remember now, you're the twins that are not twins, I haven't seen you together for some time, which one is Justin?"

Both said "I am."

The owner looked a bit shocked; he really wasn't sure what to do.

"It's ok" Ellette told the owner "Justin is our friend now, we will vouch for his good behaviour, he is a reformed character now, aren't you Justin" Justin nodded agreement.

"Ok, but no silly carry on please, ok?"

They sat at the same seats they used the last time, girls in the middle and boys on the outside, burgers were ordered, and eaten, drinks were sipped, and a lot of talking was done, and firm mutual friendships were formed. Whether they would last or not time would tell, there was still so much to learn about each other. It wasn't too late when the boys walked the girl's home.

Next decision time

On the walk home Ellette was trying to work out, kiss or no kiss, excitement was building.

"I've never been out with a boy before; you're my first date."

"Why, such a lovely girl like you?"

"I think most boys are afraid of me!

"Well, you are a very strong-willed girl, and a lot of boys want a girl that will do as she is told."

"Are you one of those as well?" she asked.

"Used to be but found those type of girls are not much fun to be with."

"Not enough of a challenge, unlike me"

"You're different in so many ways, maybe more interesting would be a better way you describe you."

"Is that a compliment?"

"I would take it as one."

"Ok, why have you changed your attitude towards me?"

"First of all, your eyes are, well they look alight, like there is a fire behind them."

"Wow, never thought of them that way."

"When we were annoying you in the alley, you seemed so positive then your eyes started to sparkle as if there was electricity behind them."

"You could be right there."

"Can you do that any time? or is it just for special occasions, like when you say protector, because every time you say that your eyes sparkle" Ellette's eyes went wide "yes just like that, what are you thinking about."

She wanted to say kissing, but she said 'protector.'

She looked over Justin's shoulder as Snowball started to form.

"How do you deal with surprises?" Ellette asked.

"I just love surprises" Justin responded.

"Well, you wanted to know what my protector was, are you ready for the biggest surprise of your life, quite literally the biggest surprise you will ever have?"

"Bring it on."

"Promise you won't scream."

"There is nothing you can do that will make me scream."

"Turn round then."

He turned round, then he screamed, stepped back, tripped over his own feet and landed on his backside in front of Ellette, looking up at a two and a half metre tall pure white Gorilla.

"Justin, meet snowball. Snowball this is Justin, say hello."

Snowball growled. Justin just sat there too shocked and stunned to say anything. Ellette whispered 'home' and Snowball evaporated.

"Wa, Wa, Wa, was that real?" Justin stuttered as he struggled to stand up.

"Yes, he's real. Told you I was different, and magical."

"That's what we bumped onto in the alley?"

"Yes"

"No wonder you didn't panic when we trapped you in the alley."

"Well, you said you wanted a girl that was different and unpredictable, so how do you feel about having a girl that is a Little Elf, which is what Ellette means?"

"At the moment I'm not sure."

"But I'm still a pretty little girl, you said so yourself" Ellette said demurely, eyes cast down.

Justin struggled to stand up from his position on the ground. Ellette held out her hand to help him, which he accepted. As he got to his feel Ellette pulled him gently towards her, then looked up shyly into his eyes. It has been told that the eyes of an elf can either freeze or melt anybody's heart. Justin's heart melted, he bent down and kissed her gently on the cheek.

"Does that mean you can accept me as I am?" she asked tentatively.

"Well, you accepted that I could change, and a relationship must work both ways, so yes, yes it does."

Ellette's smile, almost made Justin's knees quake.

"I can't wait to tell Jason all about what just happened."

"He will have his own problems dealing with Mei, she has her own special talents, maybe he has landed on his backside as well."

That was when they noticed that they were still holding hands.

Jason was having his own problems, he learned that Mie was a martial artist, as he was, so he challenged Mie to try and hit him. She didn't try, she was so fast that she actually did hit him, a bit harder than expected. He was so surprised, he lost balance and landed on his backside as well. Unusual ways for relationships to start but it seemed to work. Phone calls between the girls were exchanged after each date, learning about boys was challenging but so exciting.

Holiday time

It was going to be difficult leaving the boys for a week, Jason had been traveling back to see Mei frequently over the past few weeks, but this holiday was going to be a great experience for both Ellette and Mei.

The hotel was not large, but then again it was not small either. It had been a manor house before being converted and extended to be used as a hotel, and it had been owned by the same family for many generations. It was only about a four-hour drive from their home, so after picking up Mei, and stopping for lunch, they still arrived there in the late afternoon. Plenty of time for dinner, them a walk before it was time for bed.

But booking in to the hotel was to cause a bit of an exception. They pulled their bags from the car and headed towards the reception desk.

"Good afternoon" the receptionist said, he was a handsome young lad about eighteen years old, and full of enthusiasm. "I'm Brian, how can I help you?" he looked at Ellette and smiled.

"Mr and Mrs Avery, daughter Ellette and friend Mei Ling, we have booked two rooms."

The young lad's eyes went wide, and he took a step back from the desk.

"What's wrong, is there a problem with the booking?" Mr Avery asked.

"No" he said excitedly, his voice rising an octave "no problem with the booking, I had heard you were coming, but I did not believe it, until you told me your name" his eyes were fixed on Ellette. Then he shouted "Dad, dad you better get out here, *they have arrived*,"

A middle-aged man, the hotel owner, entered the reception area from a side door behind the desk. He saw his guests, he stopped, looking a bit unsettled.

"What is going on here" Mr Avery asked.

"Nothing, well we did not believe this would actually happen when you made the booking."

Mr Avery was looking so confused.

"You have no idea who you are, do you?" the hotel owner stated.

"I am Mr Avery, this is my wife Mrs Avery, my daughter Ellette" the owner and his son both bowed their heads towards Ellette "and her friend Mei, what is not to understand."

"Avery" stated the owner, they both bowed their heads again towards Ellette.

"What about it, Avery, that is my name" Mr Avery was starting to get a bit annoyed.

"Do you know what the name Avery means?"

"Not got a clue" Mr Avery told him.

"Elf Ruler, it means Elf Ruler, and your daughter Is Ellette, so she is Little Elf Ruler. There has been a legend passed down over the centuries about a new ruler of the Elves and Fairies coming. Now we believe that the legend is true and is about to be fulfilled" the owner said so seriously.

Mr Avery burst out laughing.

"You are winding us up, this is a marketing ploy, come on admit it."

But the owner just stood there with such a serious look on his face. Mr Avery stopped laughing.

"You cannot be serious?" he questioned.

"Has your daughter Ellette any special gifts?" the owned asked.

"How would you know that?" Mrs Avery asked.

"All part of the legend" The owned stated again.

"Dad, this is why we are here, I knew I had to come here, I have something special to do. I need to go for a walk through the Fairy Glen."

"Yes, you do, at the Fairy hour, midnight, that is your time" the owner said.

"She is not going out anywhere at midnight, especially not on her own" Mrs Avery said defiantly.

"Her rainbow will show her the way" The owner said confidently.

"How do you know about my Rainbow" Ellette asked him.

"All part of the legend, but I have no idea how you will see a rainbow in the dark?"

"**My** Rainbow can see in the dark" Ellette said.

"Your Rainbow is not a **thing**; it is an **IT**?"

"Would you like to see him?" Ellette asked.

"I have been here for many years. I was here when you were here the first time, and I remember your daughter being born, it was said then that she had been visited by Fairies, but I've never seen a Fairy, or anything magical" the owner said. "I'm not sure if I should, I'm not sure if I am ready?" he was looking enquiringly at Mr Avery.

"We were both there when she was born, and we never saw any fairies either, we have never seen her Rainbow before either."

Mei was standing giggling; she knew what was coming.

Ellette looked around, there was nobody else about, so she called 'Rainbow'.

Multi coloured mist formed next to her, finally taking the form of Rainbow, her full-sized rainbow coloured tiger. Ellette put her hand on his head and scratched his ear. He purred in pleasure; well, it was more of a deep rumble than a purr. Mei was jumping about and clapping her hands with joy, everyone else was too shocked or too scared to move.

"My boyfriend fell on his backside when he saw my protector for the first time."

The owner's son looked a bit dejected on hearing she already had a boyfriend.

"No, Ellette we don't want to see your protector, this space is too small for him to fit in" her mum said.

"Protector?" the owner enquired.

"You really don't want to know" replied Mrs Avery.

"How about Hairy knees then?"

"NO" her mum and dad said firmly,

"Just asking" Ellette said with a cheeky smile.

Mei looked a bit disappointed.

"Does that mean I can go for my walk at midnight then?" Ellette asked.

"I suppose so, as long as you are careful, you never know who will be out there" her mum told her.

"And Mei can come with me?"

"Am I going to get see Elves and Fairies?" Mei asked while jumping up and down, she was almost crying with excitement.

"You were the baby we saw when first came here almost eighteen years ago" Ellette's mum said to the young man, she was trying to calm the situation and bring things back to some sort of normality. "How about we get our keys, drop off our bags, and then we can all go for a walk, and talk this thing through, before we have dinner" endeavouring to be the voice of reason.

The register was signed, keys were handed over, luggage was dropped in their rooms, they met again in the reception area, the time for their evening meal was agreed and booked, the weather was fine and mild, so time for the walk of a lifetime, until the next time.

"You already know where you are going, so enjoy" The owner told them.

The made their way out the back door of the hotel,

"Wow!" Ellette stopped and gazed in wonder at the scene in front of her.

The back door of the hotel led on to a large walled garden. Because of the ambiance of the garden many people liked to eat outside, therefor there was a large patio area set out with tables and chairs, beyond that there was a beautiful flower garden, planted with flowers of every different colour you could think of, and beyond that, was a large well-kept vegetable garden. But the main feature, was the furthest away, the garden wall was three metre's tall, and at the end of the path leading from the back door was a two-metre-tall arched door set in the wall, it looked about the size of a toy Fairy door. A voice behind them said 'don't believe your eyes' It was the owners voice. Just before the door was an arch covered in White Wisteria in full bloom, which seemed to shine in the afternoon sunshine, and hanging from the arch was a sign saying 'Fairy Glen' the whole space seemed to shout there is magic all around you.

"No wonder you talked about this place so much it's just so beautiful, why didn't we come here for holidays before now?" Ellette queried.

"We had our reasons; we wanted you to be ready. What you are about to see is, well, overpowering to say the least, and we knew how passionate and excitable you are about Fairies, so we waited till you asked" Her mum said.

They walked along the path, Ellette was so focused on the door, but when they reached the flower garden the smell of the different flowers was so strong, they had to pause and enjoy the experience. The vegetables looked to fresh, and wholesome, it made them hungry just looking at them. Finally, standing under the Wisteria arch they reached the door, which was closed. The door was in two halves, opening from the middle and hinged at either side.

"Right girls"

"Muuum, we're not girls anymore."

"Well, you will always be girls to me" she stated. "Take a handle each and pull the door open."

The door swung open, revealing a wide path leading away from the door on the other side of the wall, the path went both right and left.

"The Glen is set out in a loop so you can go either way and the path will bring you back here" Mrs Avery started to get very emotional, so many good memories, Mr Avery held her hand.

"Mum, Dad, not here please"

"We can hold hands any time we want and now seems appropriate to do so" Mr Avery stated firmly.

There were trees, so many trees that you could not see very far ahead, there were bushes, and wildflowers of all kinds wherever you looked, the sun was shining through the taller trees, dappled sunlight danced on the undergrowth, it truly looked and felt like a Fairy Glen. They entered, then closed the door behind them, silence was everywhere, time seemed to vanish, it was as if somebody had just switched on the magic. They turned left and walked slowly along the path which led them down into a shallow valley with a gurgling stream running through it. They stood on the bridge that crossed the stream, listening to the sound of the water. On the far side of the bridge a narrow road approached from the left-hand side.

"Mum?"

"Yes Ellette, that is where the ambulance came to get me when I went in to labour, it all happened so quickly, this is where you were born."

"MAGIC" Mei whispered; she was totally captivated by the whole situation. "Where are the Fairies and the Elves?" she asked, looking around.

"They are here, I can feel them, but they are not yet ready to show themselves, later, will be the time, we should be getting back, I have some learning to do" Ellette told them.

They made their way back to the hotel and found that they had been away for over an hour, time started again, dinner time had arrived. Ellette had already learned that there was a small library in the hotel with books about the history of the hotel and about the legend of the Fairy Glen. After dinner she spent time alone reading.

Decision Time again

Midnight was approaching, darkness was creeping over the land. The girls were excited and more than a little anxious. Mei, Ellette and her parents were standing before the closed door.

"Are you sure you want to go through with this?" her mum asked Ellette.

"Yes and no, but it's something I need to do, this is the next step in my life as Little Elf" she whispered 'Rainbow' and he appeared, standing between herself and Mei.

"Time" Ellette said, they reached forward and pulled the doors open, darkness engulfed them, then Rainbow started to glow, giving

Ellette confidence to take the first step through the door into the glen, the doors then closed behind them.

"It's so dark I can't see a thing" Mei said anxiously.

"It's not that dark, Rainbow is the colour of light, he is giving of enough light to see by, I can see quite well."

"I can't see a thing; we need to go back and get a torch."

"Why can I see, and you can't?"

"Maybe it's because you are magic and I'm not."

"Oh, Ok, Eh, close your eyes, Mei, let me try something."

Mei closed her eyes, Ellette put her hands over her closed eyes and whispered 'Fairy Sight' then took her hands away.

"Now open your eyes, tell me what you see?"

Mei opened her eyes very slowly; it sounded as if the whole wood sighed.

"Wow, did you hear that? Wow, Rainbow is so bright Look at all the colours, I can see every detail of everything, did you just do magic on me?"

"I guess so, remember I am still learning."

"Are there Elves and Fairies about?"

"I think it was them sighing when I did my magic on you. We need to go down to the bridge, that is the heart of the glen" they started to walk slowly down the path, there was sounds coming from the trees all around them.

"Is that why you are so special, because you were born near the heart of the glen?"

"Partly, our family history has been linked to this place for a long time."

"Does that mean that your whole family is magic?"

"No, only me, there seems to be something more special about me that I don't know about yet."

"Spooky" Mei giggled. "What do Elves and Fairies look like?" she asked.

"Pretty much like they do in the pictures in children's books, somebody a long time ago knew the Fairies and Elves and drew pictures of them."

"Could it have been one of your ancestors?"

"Yes, it was, hundreds of year ago one of our family was accepted by them as an Elf Friend, that is when the legend started. They were given Fairy powers, but she could not use them because she would have been called a Witch and killed, so the power has lain dormant, till now. It's all written down in one of the oldest books in the library, it's written in ancient Elvish, but I can read it" the wood sighed again.

They had reached to bridge.

"I am here to claim my rightful place" Ellette called.

"What gives you the right?" A voice questioned.

"When I was born, I was given the Magic of the Fairies and the Wisdom of the Elves" she stated with confidence.

"Who was that and where are they?" Mei asked.

"Come, show yourselves" Ellette demanded "we are all friends here."

A figure moved out from the tree line at the other end of the bridge.

"Wow" Mei exclaimed "is that an Elf, they are sure ugly" Mei said as she cowered behind Ellette.

"Tell me what you see Mei."

"He, I think it's a he? He looks like he's made out of mud, about one and a half metres tall, long black unkempt hair, long dirty looking black beard, and the ugliest face I have ever seen, he looks so evil, like one of those goblins you see in some films."

"That is what he wants you to see, he actually looks nothing like that" Ellette put her hand on Mei's shoulder "close your eyes and use your Fairy sight" she did what she was asked "now open your eyes and tell me what you see now."

"So beautiful, he's dressed in a long silvery gown, long silky golden hair and a face that seems to shine."

"He is an Elf high lord" she bowed slowly towards him he returned the bow.

"I have read the old books, I know why I am here at this time, and I have the power." Ellette stated.

"What makes you think you have the power required for the task?"

Ellette whispered 'home' Rainbow disappeared. She focused all her power then shouted.

"Protector"

White mist formed on the path behind her. Then grew and grew and grew, until it reached to same height as the trees, then formed into a massive white Gorilla, Snowball had arrived.

"Told you I have the power" she said quietly smiling.

"Ellette, what task are you talking about?" Mei asked.

"Humans" The Elf lord answered, "the places we live in, the magical creatures, are being put under pressure by human expansion, and the planet is being damaged by human rubbish, we need someone to fight for our space in the human world."

"I am only seventeen years old, well almost eighteen, why would they listen to me?"

"We, the ancient magical creatures, have lived in this world long before humans took over, always hiding from them because of the way they treated and persecuted us, apart from the humans that were our Elf friends. We are finding, that hiding, is not going to work for much longer."

"You said WE the magical creatures, what do you mean by magical creatures?" Mei asked.

"Do you think that Fairy tales are built on myth, on people thinking and using their imagination? Wrong, Unicorns, Fairies, Leprechauns, the Loch Ness Monster, Big Foot, the Yeti, Centaur, the Phoenix, and many others are all real, but they hide from humans because they are hunted and persecuted."

"You are just kidding me, aren't you?" Mei's eyes went wide "The Gruffalo as well?" Mei said excitedly.

"No, the Gruffalo is modern made-up creature."

"Vampires and Werewolves?"

"Same again made up to scare people."

"OK" Mei accepted. "Just like you made yourself look scary to try and scare me."

"Yes. Now come forward my friends" lights appeared from behind the trees. More Elves appeared, as well as Fairies with small lanterns who flew out and landed on the high lord's shoulders. More Fairies followed, leading fawns and riding on the back of unicorns, along with them came all the animals and birds of the forest.

Ellette whispered 'home' and Snowball faded away, then she called 'Lightning' he appeared and stood next to her.

"Magnificent, the most magical of all creatures" the high Elf bowed to Lightning who lowered his head in return. The other unicorns made their way to greet Lightning.

"You truly have the power we require. When you are eighteen you will become the Queen and ruler of **all** ancient and magical creatures"

"Whoa, not so fast, I'm not ready for anything like that, did you just say **all** magical creatures?"

"You stated when you arrived that you were here to claim your rightful place, you already have the magic of the Fairies and you will learn the wisdom of the Elves, your rightful place is Queen, that is why you are here."

"I don't know about all my powers yet."

"You will not receive your full powers until you become of age, at eighteen of your years, at that time you will understand, and learn so much more of our ways. You will need time to prepare. The sun is rising, it is almost dawn, you should return to your other family, come back again tonight as the sun goes down, we have many things to discuss."

Darkness folded over them for a second. Ellette called for Rainbow to give them light, when Rainbow arrived, they found that all the magical creatures had vanished.

"What an experience, I can't wait to tell everybody about what happened tonight" Mei said excitedly, she was a very excitable young woman.

"You can't tell anybody about this, not yet anyway. We need to find out what is going to happen to me when I turn eighteen in a few weeks' time."

The sun was rising as they walked back to the door, they talked about everything that had happened, just to confirm that it actually had happened.

"You've been away for hours" her mum commented as they opened the door "what happened?"

Ellette gave them a brief outline of the meeting with the magical creatures.

"**You are going to be a Fairy Queen**?" her mum said excitedly "**and I'm going to be a Queen Mum,** oh I think I'm going to faint, this is so exciting."

"I have to visit them each day for the rest of the holiday, to get more information about what they want from me. I also have a feeling that they want Mei to be there as well."

"Why would they want me there, do they want me to do something as well?"

"There is only one way to find out."

They continued to visit the Fairies and Elves each day. Mei found out that she was to be Ellette's companion in the forthcoming adventure. She was so excited. She just loved to play with the Fairies and ride on the back of the unicorns.

The holiday was over quicker than they thought, time flies when you are having fun, and they had lots of fun in the Fairy Glen getting to know all about the Magical Creatures.

Final step

They continued to work in the Pet shop. it was difficult not to say too much about the holiday when they were out with their respective boyfriends.

Ellette's eighteenth birthday arrived, the night before her birthday she was so anxious, she had no idea what to expect.

The household was woken early the next morning by Ellette shouting.

"I've got wings."

PART 4

FAIRY QUEEN ELF

Joyous are those who accept
they are different.

Queen Ellette

Final Awakening

Six o'clock in the morning, still in her pyjamas, Ellette rushed into her mum and dad's Bedroom after shouting **'I've got wings.'**

"Luckily we don't have any neighbours" they lived in a detached house "or else they might have thought you had been drinking something, just what do you mean by I've got wings?" her mum asked.

Ellette turned round to show that the back of her pyjama top was ripped open. She turned back to face her mum and dad.

"Watch" she said, multi coloured double butterfly wings started to unfurl through the tear in her pyjamas. When they were fully unfurled, they were about two metres across from tip to tip, and they started just above the floor and almost reached the ceiling.

"I was told to expect something on my eighteenth birthday, but this it totally awesome. What do you think of them?"

Her mum and dad were speechless, again. Over the last few years Ellette had given them so many unexpected and amazing surprises.

"They're going to take a bit of hiding" her dad exclaimed.

"They roll up very small, I can wear a halter top and a baggy jacket over it, no one will ever know, but I don't have halter top, well not yet anyway. I need to go shopping."

"Next question" her mum asked, "why do you have wings?"

"I am now the Queen of all magical creatures on the earth" She stated.

"And just what does that mean exactly?"

"I have to take on the human world to win a place for the magical creatures."

"I thought that Elves don't have wings, only Fairies and Sprites have wings."

"But I am special. I was given a magical gift by both Elves and Fairies, therefor I am both Fairy and Elf. I need to find somewhere I can practice using them. Daaaad, can you drive me over to the forest this morning please?"

"I suppose so" her resigned dada said.

"I need to go and call Mei, boy is she going to scream."

She screamed, then followed a long phone call.

"Mei wants to come with me to the forest. Can we go and pick her up please?"

"I've got work to go to" her dad stated.

"You can leave us there and I can fly home."

"What about other people seeing you?" her mum said.

One second Ellette was standing in front of her, the next second, she was gone, well not gone but gone from sight.

"I can make myself invisible to anybody I want, not just those that don't believe."

Again, her dad was speechless.

They went to pick up Mei, she was standing on the pavement, well not really standing, she was jumping up and down with excitement. Mr Ling was standing beside her trying to calm her down and not succeeding.

"Remember, work as normal, or as normal as you two can be, at nine o'clock." He said calmly.

"Watch the skies for us Mr Ling" Ellette said laughingly.

Mr Avery found the drive to the forest very trying, the two girls were either laughing or talking, there was no half measure with them. At last, they arrived at a clearing in the forest, the girls got out the car, Ellette took of her jacket, she had cut the back out on one of her tops, she unfurled her wings, and Mei let out the loudest and most piercing scream Mr Avery had ever heard.

Ellette bounced on her toes a few times to get the feel of her wings, then she bounced higher, flapped her wings and took off like a rocket. Ellette screamed with pure joy, she had never known such freedom. She flew round in a large circle then landed again, beside the car.

"That was just so much fun."

"Did you catch any flies up there" her dad said with a smile, just to wind her up.

"Dad, that's not Funnee" she said in an American accent, just to wind hm up, he was not a fan of American comedies.

"Can I go to work then? He asked.

"Just one more thig before you go, Mei, turn round."

"Why?" she asked.

"Do you want to fly?" Ellette smiled, and Mei nodded.

Mei turned round, Ellette put her arms round her, jumped, flapped her wings, and soared into the sky. Mei Screamed again.

"I just wanted to know what weight I could carry, Bye dad" Mei waved at Mr Avery, she was glad that Ellette had not tried to wave as well.

"Can things get any more insane with those two" Mr Avery shook his head as he got back into the car. He had no idea.

Unexpected Meeting

As they were about to leave the forest and fly back to the shop, Ellette noticed an unusual disturbance at the base of one of the trees, she flew down to investigate. They landed a short distance from the tree and were walking towards it when a figure appeared. A High wood Elf approached them, High Elves are the oldest Elves in the colony, and can be either male or female, he stopped then bowed. Ellette returned the bow.

"Do you have orders for me?" Ellette asked.

"I would never be so bold as to give my Queen orders. My presence here is not for my Queen, it is for Mei I am here."

Mei looked very anxious and unsettled.

"What do the Elves want with me?" She asked.

"You have been accepted as an Elf Friend. This honour is only given to those who have a pure heart. We have a gift to bestow on you, to enhance your natural powers we give you the gift of Fairy speed, and Elf wisdom, these are given because of your friendship and support of our Queen Ellette, and also because she will need your support and guidance in the future, remember these powers are not for you, they are given for the good of all."

Mei did not scream this time, but Ellette did, she was so pleased for her friend.

"I thank you for your gracious gift, can you tell me how fast?"

"You will find out, when required. I will leave you now, with one more piece of information about our magical community, Elves believe in Peace and Humility, Fairies and Sprites believe in Peace and Mischief, all others believe in Peace and Freedom, there is no room for arrogance, greed, violence or retribution in our magical community, bear well this information because others will try take you down that forbidden path"

The flight back to the shop was exciting but uneventful, apart from laughing at people looking up at the sky when they heard the beating of Ellette's wings, they looked so confused. Ellette landed in the alley behind the shop, Mei knocked on the door, which was soon opened by her dad.

"Well, tell me what happened then" he asked.

"You're not going to believe this dad."

"I know Ellette can fly, you've already told me."

"This is not about Ellette, it's about me. we met a high Elf, I am now an Elf Friend, and I have been given a gift, the gift of speed."

"Do you know what form the speed will take?"

"Not yet, the High Elf said I will find out!

"Ok, Ellette you will need to find a way of hiding these wings, very quickly, we have visitors in the shop that are very keen to see the two of you."

"NO, not yet, is it Justin and Jason?" Ellette asked anxiously.

"Who else would it be?"

Ellette quickly folded away her wings then put on her white coat she wore when working in the shop, then they quickly brushed their hair, flying really upsets your hair style, before going through to meet the boys.

"Happy Birthday" the boys called as Ellette entered the shop.

There was hugs and kissed all round. After Justin pulled back from hugging Ellette he said.

"Ellette what are you wearing under your coat, it feels like something that is rolled up?"

Ellette blushed "I can't tell you right now, it's a surprise" she stammered.

"A Birthday surprise?" he asked.

"You could call it that" she told him.

"A BIG surprise?" the last big surprise was when he saw Snowball, Ellette's white Gorilla.

"Yes"

"Bigger that the last one?" he said uncertainly.

"Oh yes" she smiled.

"But a good one?"

"All depends on what you define as good."

Justin looked a bit apprehensive "Will I find out later what it is?"

"Oh! You will definitely find out."

"OK, can't wait, Birthday meal tonight, our treat?"

The girls looked at each other, smiled then nodded.

"Good, we will pick you up at home about seven o'clock, that ok?"

"That will be perfect, it will give me time to do some shopping, eh, can I ask a favour, could you pick up Mei before you come for me please."

"Ok" the boys looked a bit confused as they left the shop.

"Now this could be a bit tricky" Mr Ling exclaimed.

They left the shop earlier than normal, shopping was done, time to get home and get ready for whatever was going to unfold.

'Bing Bong' seven o'clock the doorbell rang. Mr Avery went to answer it; they had already met the boys.

"Come this way" he ushered them into the living room. As they entered the room Justin saw Ellette.

"Wow! Ellette you look stunning" he said.

She was wearing a bright red, brand new, halter top with trousers and shoes to match.

Jason had already complimented on Mei on her outfit.

"Ready for the surprise?" Ellette asked.

"Yes" Justin said excitedly.

Ellette unfurled her multi coloured butterfly wings. Justin got such a shock that he stepped back, bumped into Jason knocked him over, and they both fell on to their backsides. Both girls laughed.

"Now there's something we haven't see before" Ellette said between laughs.

"You can say that again" Jason said, still a bit shocked.

"What on earth is going on, I know you told me you were special, but just who are you?" Justin asked.

"I am Ellette, Queen of the Elves and Fairies and every magical creature on the earth."

Jason looked at Mei as if to say 'is this real' Mei just smiled and nodded.

"Magic isn't it" she said. "and I am her right hand, whatever is required."

"Do you have magical powers as well?" Jason queried.

"Magical no, I'm just super-fast."

"How fast" he asked.

"Not sure yet, still to find out."

Back to reality.

"I don't know about you but I sure am hungry. Are we still going out for that meal you promised?" Ellette asked.

"Sure, sure, fine, no problem" the boys were still a bit shell shocked.

Ellette put on a baggy red jacket and they made their way out to Jason's car.

After they had left the house Mr Avery murmured to himself 'poor boys'

The time

The company was friendly, the food was excellent, and devoured quickly, the conversation was mostly one sided, the girls had a lot to say, some things never change.

"What did you say you had to do Ellette" Justin queried.

"I have to get the human race to agree to accept that magical creatures have a place in this world, and they should not be persecuted or hunted because they are different."

"So, you are going to show yourself in public in all your Fairy Elvish glory, wings and everything?"

"Shush, yes, I am, when the time is right."

"And Mei is going to help you" Jason said.

"YES, I am." Mei stated proudly.

"Is that not going to be dangerous? Some people are not going to accept that, they will try and fight you."

"That is why I have my special powers, but I will not fight, there is no violence among the magical creatures, and I am now one of those."

There was a loud crash outside the restaurant, a few seconds later the door of the burst open and somebody shouted. 'We need help out here, there's been a terrible crash, a child is trapped under a truck.'

Mei looked at Ellette and nodded, the *time* had arrived.

The four of them rushed out to see what had happened, it appeared that the trucks brakes had failed, and it had mounted the pavement where an eight year old girl had been standing, a few feet from her mum, the trucks tyres had burst when it hit the high kerb. It had not crushed the girl but she was pinned underneath it. People were talking to her, she was not badly injured, but she was bleeding and needed urgent medical help, she was screaming and crying, and understandably she was starting to panic.

"The fire brigade can't get here for at least ten minutes, what can we do?" somebody shouted.

Ellette whispered 'Protector'.

Snowball started to appear, most of the onlookers started to panic as well, well who wouldn't if you say a two and a half metre tall white gorilla start to appear out of nowhere.

Snowball looked at Ellette "Lift the truck Snowball" she said softly.

He put his great hands under the side of the truck and heaved. The side of the truck was now high enough for somebody to crawl under and pull the girl out, but nobody seemed brave enough to go near, let alone go under the truck.

Justin and Jason dived under the truck and gently pulled her to safety. It seems they were now part of the Ellette entourage. She was given first aid for her injuries, cuts and bruises and a broken arm, she was complaining of pain in her chest. At this point the ambulance arrived and took over her treatment. The police arrived and moved everybody back from around the girl and the ambulance crew. After a short time Ellette sensed that there was a problem.

"Is there a problem" she asked a policeman.

"She has chest injuries, and needs to get to the hospital very quickly, but the ambulance has broken down,"

"I can help, can I speak to the ambulance crew please,"

He looked at her as if to say' how can you help' but he called one of the paramedics over.

Ellette took him to the side and talked to him in whispers, he looked shocked and apprehensive.

"Please, I can help, a police car can't get her there quickly enough, but I can" she pleaded.

He called over the girl's mum, told her what Ellette suggested, she as well looked shocked.

"Can I talk to her" Ellette asked. The mum nodded.

They escorted Ellette over to where the injured girl was.

"Hi, my name is Ellette, what is yours,"

"Emily" she whispered.

"Emily, do you believe in Fairies?"

"Yes" with a faint smile "I do, are you a Fairy?"

"I am more than that, I am a Fairy Queen?"

The girl's eyes went wide in surprise.

"You need to get to the hospital very quickly, if you like I can fly you there, the police will take your mum there in their car"

"Ok" Emily said quietly.

Ellette took a deep breath, took of her jacket and unfurled her wings. The crowd gasped and took another step back in shock.

Somebody had to do it, somebody shouted 'Freak,'

Ellette ignored the negative comment. The paramedics lifted Emily into Ellette's arms.

"Let them know I am on my way, which was is the hospital?" The paramedic pointed out the direction.

Ellette took a step forward, jumped, flapped ger wings, soared over the crowd then the rooftops and headed in the direction pointed out to her.

One police officer drove away with Emily's mum, the other approached Mei and the two boys.

"I think you have some explaining to do?" they all smiled nervously, thinking we did not expect things to happen this way or so quickly.

Ellette got to the hospital in three minutes, it would have taken a police car at least ten times longer. She landed at the entrance to the A&E department. There was already a team of doctors and nurses waiting for them. Emily was put on a trolley and quickly wheeled inside. One of the senior nurses waited outside with Ellette.

They stood for a few seconds, just watching each other.

"My name is Matilda, most people call me Matty, and you are?" the senior nurse asked.

"I am Ellette, Queen of the Elves, and Fairies" she added.

Matilda then said something in a very unusual language, but Ellette understood exactly what she was saying.

"You can speak ancient Elvish" Ellette was totally astounded.

"I am an Elf Friend, I heard about the legend, but not that it had come true. Tell me what has happened."

"I only turned eighteen today, I woke up with these wings this morning. I have had meetings with the high Elves, and they told me that it was time for all Magical creatures to be accepted as part of the world, and I am to be the one to make it happen."

"That is quite a task for one so young."

"It was thought that an older person would have their own agenda, and that a younger person would be more openminded. I have known I was magical for a few years now, but only reach my real potential this morning. Quite a birthday present don't you think?"

"A lot of humans will resent your powers; they will either want to take your powers or destroy you; you will need to be very careful."

"I have other human friends that will be there to help me."

"Can I ask a favour before the authorities come and take you away?"

"Please ask Matilda, I am here to serve."

"We have many sick children in the hospital. Can you come and say hello to them?"

"I would be delighted to, please lead the way, wings out or away?"

"With wings as beautiful as you have, they must be out. The children will be so excited."

The expressions on the adults faces as she walked the hospital corridors was priceless. As they entered the paediatric area, one young boy, about five years old, was holding his mum's hand, he shouted 'are you a Fairy?' Ellette stopped bent down, his mum backed away.

"No, I'm an Elvish Queen, and a Fairy, and I'm called Ellette, what is your name."

"I'm Billy. Can you do fairy magic things?" he asked. Ellette nodded. "Can you show me some magic, please."

His mum looked very apprehensive; children deal with unusual situations better than most adults.

"Are you sick?" Ellette asked, the boy nodded "I have something that can make you feel better. Have you ever cuddled a Gorilla or stroked a Tiger?"

"No, can I?" he asked excitedly.

"What one would you like to do?"

"Tiger please, a real size, full real size tiger" Billy said.

Ellette whispered 'Rainbow.'

As Rainbow started to form all the adults tried to back away, but the young boy held his ground, his eyes were so wide.

"Go on stroke him, he likes it."

"Will he eat me?" he asked.

"No, he will not eat you, he does not eat anything."

"What does he live on then?"

"LOVE Billy, he lives on love."

The boy reached over and stroked Rainbows ear, Rainbow started with his loud deep purr, he sounded so happy.

"Anybody else want to stroke him?" Ellette asked, all the adults backed away even further, most adults have an un-natural aversion to things that are different, or that they don't understand. Except for the Matilda. She knelt down and wrapped her arms round Rainbows neck. He nuzzled into her embrace.

"Can your magic make sick people well again?" Billy asked.

"I'm sorry but it can't, but it can make you feel better, have you heard of Fairy dust?"

"I've heard of it, but I don't know what it is, do you have some?"

Ellette pulled a small bag from her belt.

"You can't give that child medication and get that animal out of here," a voice from behind dictated, it was the senior registrar, the big boss, he was big in size as well, almost two metres tall and weighed well over one hundred kilos. She whispered to Billy 'he sounds like an Ogre' Billy laughed.

Ellette stood up and turned round, she would not be dominated by his aggression or his size "It's not medication it's only Fairy dust,"

"What's in it then?" he demanded. Matilda rolled her eyes.

"Nothing happens in here without me knowing about it,"

Matilda whispered to Ellette 'will it work on him?'

Ellette smiled, then she took a small pinch from the bag, and put it on the palm of her hand which she held out, so that he could see what it was. As he bent down, she gently blew the dust into his face. He looked very angry, then he relaxed, smiled, turned and walked slowly away.

"I'll need to get me some of that, that's stuffs magic" Matilda said.

Decision time once more

An idea was forming within Ellette's mind, but she would need time to think the idea through. Her thought process was disturbed by Mei shouting "Hi" she was slightly out of breath.

"Where's the boys?" Ellette queried.

"Following in the police car" She smiled "I ran, thought I would try out my gift, he, he, that was fun, how is Emily?"

"Haven't heard yet, Mei this Matilda" They both said 'Hi' "she is also an Elf Friend,"

"I bet the children just love your calling your name" Mei commented. Matilda nodded and smiled.

"Matilda can you find out how Emily is please?"

"No problem, back in a minute"

She walked over the nurse's station, spoke softly to the nurse in charge who picked up a phone, talked for a short time then hung up, she was smiling as she talked to Matilda, who was smiling as she walked over to Mei and Ellette.

"She is fine, children are so resilient, she has bruised ribs and a broken arm, she is getting a plaster on just now, then she will be sent up here to our ward, for an overnight for observations."

The news of Ellette's arrival had spread, small heads were looking round the doors of the rooms in the children's ward.

Ellette waved, then flapped her wings, there was screams of delight coming from every room.

"I want to see them all, but first who Is the sickest child here?"

Matilda led Ellette to a small single room, lying in the bed was a five year old girl, she was barely conscious, and did not look well at all. Her mum was sitting beside her holding her hand.

"I wondered what all the commotion was, I know somebody shouted 'Fairy' I had no idea there was a real one. You are a Fairy. Aren't you?" the girls mum asked.

"Fairy Queen, real fairies are much smaller, Hi, what is your name" she asked the girl.

"Tina" she whispered.

"Hi, Tina, my name is Ellette. "Can I give her something to make her feel better" Ellette asked her mum.

"Can you cure her" she asked.

"I'm sorry, that's one thing I can't do, but I can help her feel better" she took out the fairy dust bag and sprinkled some on Tina's head" Tina smiled for the first time in months, her mum smiled then cried with joy.

"If that stuff can make kids feel better, then I'll have some of it" Mr Ogre the registrar grabbed the bag from Ellette.

"Won't do you any good, it won't work for you. It's not the dust that is magic, it's the Fairies that use it, go on try it on somebody/"

He grabbed the nearest nurse and through some in her face.

"What do you think you are playing at" She scolded. Then walked away muttering under her breath.

"Told you, now can I have it back, please?"

A bit disgruntled, but he handed it back to her.

"There's somebody here to see you" Mei said to Ellette.

Emily was being wheeled along the corridor by one of the porters, her mum was walking beside her.

"Have you been looked after Emily?" Ellette asked.

"Yes, I have, everybody has been so nice, lots of people have been asking what it was like to fly here, I just told them it was so much fun."

"I don't know how you did what you did for Emily, I don't know how to thank you" Emily's mum was so grateful and emotional that she burst into tears.

Ellette walked up to her and gave her a hug.

"You don't need to thank us. I am just happy that we were there to help her. I think she will be a major celebrity during her overnight stay."

"Oh Oh, here comes trouble" Mei said. The boys were walking towards them being led by two police officers.

As they got closer the boys pushed past the officers and hugged the girls.

"I suppose you want us to come with you for questioning?" Ellette asked.

"Yes, there are some very senior people who want to ask you some questions."

"Well, they can wait we have lots more children to cheer up"

"They want us to take you to them **now**" the officers took a step forward. The two boys stood in front of Ellette.

"This is the attitude that made the magical creatures stay hidden for so long, demanding what YOU want, instead of doing the right thing."

"And just what is the right thing?"

"Come with me and watch the reaction of the children when the see us."

Ellette led them into Tina's room, her little face lit up with pure joy.

"What have you done to her?" One of the officers asked.

"Made her feel happy, that's all, and we can do that to all the other children as well, its' not Magic, or well yes it is, it's how children **feel** when they think of Fairies."

They spent the next hour or so spending time with the sick children, even the police officers were feeling better just watching the reaction of the children to Ellette's visit. When it was time to leave all the children that were mobile gathered round Ellette for a final hug.

"We have to leave now, but I promise we will come back, I have one more thing to do before we leave" she whispered 'Lightning' and there he stood in all his Silver Unicorn glory, the children shrieked with joy.

Even the parents that were there with their sick children were overcome with gratitude.

Confrontation

Somebody had been very busy, as they exited the hospital, there was flashing lights everywhere, so many people were taking photos, and a television crew was waiting for them, the television people had not been allowed inside the hospital.

The news reporter was approaching them, Ellette thought for a few seconds, then took the initiative.

"Is this going out live" She asked.

"Yes, on every station, and it's also on the world wide satellite network" the reporter confirmed.

Ellette turned to the camera.

"My name is Ellette" she stated with confidence, wings flapping in the light breeze "Elven Queen of the Fairies, I represent all the magical creatures of this world. They have been hiding from the human race, they fear being persecuted and hunted because they are different. In every country of the world there are Elves, Fairies, Centaurs, Fawns, Leprechauns, Unicorns and many more."

Somebody shouted 'fraud, it's all fake, these things don't exist.'

Ellette said 'Lightning, Snowball, Rainbow' they all appeared.

"Whoever said that please come forward and see for yourself just how real these friends of mine are. If you don't have the courage, then please be quiet. These two police officers have spent the last few hours with me cheering up the sick children in this hospital, will you trust them" She turned to the officers "Have either you ridden a horse?"

"I have, what do you want me to do?" One of them answered.

"Get on lightnings back and ride him round the car park."

"You are kidding?"

"Nope, he will not let you fall off, he is so gentle."

As she said this the small boy, Billy and his mum, came out of the hospital door, without any hesitation he walked up to Rainbow and gave him a huge hug. The crowd gasped.

"It's ok" Billy said to the crowd as the microphone was pushed towards him. "He is my friend, and he loves getting his ears tickled" Rainbow purred loudly.

"There is no violence or aggression in any magical creature, anybody want to come and cuddle my Gorilla Snowball?" Matilda appeared at her shoulder, walked up to Snowball who towered over her. Snowball lifted his arms so that Matilda could get closer, then they hugged.

"He is so strong, but also so soft and gentle" Matilda commented.

This gave the Police Officer the confidence to get on Lightnings back. Lightning lowered himself so that he could be mounted, then he pranced round the car park. After the Officer dismounted, Lightning stood I front of him and bowed, as if to say thank you, the Officer returned the bow.

"He is so strong, but also so gentle, there is no aggression in him, what a lovely animal" the Officed told the crowd.

"Is that the Gorilla that lifted the truck earlier on this evening?" Someone in the crowd shouted, "Can he do it again?"

"Snowball, lift up the police car."

He walked over to the police car, after letting go of Matilda, put his hands under the front of the car and lifted it as high as he could, then he walked his hands forward till he found the balance point, then he lifted the car above his head. The crowd cheered, she was winning them over.

"Can you tell us why you are here?" The interviewer asked.

Ellette turned to the interviewer "We are here to help, we cannot fix the world's problems, but we will help in any way we can. If we had not helped at the truck crash this evening Emily could have died. We, mainly the Fairies and Elves wish to be accepted as part of the peoples of this earth. We do not want to be exploited or put in zoos or experimented on."

When they had exited the Hospital, the crowd numbered about one hundred, now it was more than ten times that many, people want to get close to the extraordinary, and when crowds gather, so does trouble. Someone at the back of the crowd shouted, 'go home freak' and a bottle was thrown towards Ellette.

"Mei time" Mei shouted, as she caught the bottle. Obviously, there was more than one trouble maker in the crowd as more missiles flew towards Ellette, which Mei caught, some of them were eggs, she thought 'Eggs who would bring eggs to a crowed place'. Mei was in her element, at last she had the chance to user her elven gift. She was running about, and sometimes jumping to catch al the missiles, and yes, she was so excited she was screaming with joy.

"Fairies" Ellette called, and a dozen Fairies appeared, flying round her head, they were about fifteen centimetre high with wings like fluttering damsel flies. "Go dust them" she told them and the Fairies quickly sprinkled Fairy dust over the group of people throwing the missiles. "That is how we deal with violence, by showing them how bad they were, then showing them how good they can be. My people and I don't want to be where we're not wanted."

"But you haven't really told us why you are here" The interviewer asked again.

"Magical creatures have lived on earth longer than any living human, our high Elves are more than ten thousand years old, we take nothing from the earth, we live with the earth, and always have done, unlike humans who try to change things to suit themselves. We can teach the human race how to live and grow food without pesticides and live without plastic. We can help you heal the planet, but it needs to be done **now**. To those of you who doubt who we are, see this" Ellette raised her voice "in every country on earth Magical Creatures show yourselves."

Elves, Fairies, Unicorns, and many other creatures appeared in every Government building, and in every public place throughout the earth, there were hundreds of them standing round Ellette.

"Children are the future of the earth, and wherever they are we can make them happy, because they believe in magic, we **can** give this troubled world a real feel good factor, this has already been proven inside the hospital. The decision to accept us should be taken by all the ordinary people of earth, not just by the governments, I am now asking all the people of earth if you want our help to make this world a better place to live in RAISE YOUR VOICE, AND SAY **YES**" SHE SHOUTED. Her voice resounded in every country around the whole world.

There were now television crews recording this earth-shattering event all over the planet.

The people of the earth responded with a resounding **'YES.'**

"Governments of the world please listen" Ellette pleaded "the people have spoken."

Over the next few days the news media was full of pictures and reports of Ellette and her Magical creatures. Governments had no choice but to accept their help, they were put under so much pressure from ordinary people, especially children.

Over the next few years Ellette, Mei and their two boys, well young men, travelled the world as ambassadors of the magical creatures, and helping to promote a better way of life.

Taking part in charity events and teaching the human race about magical creatures. They got home to work in the pet shop occasionally. Both couples got married and had families of their own, the twin gene carried on to the next generation, both couples had twins, boys for Mei and girls for Ellette, not much fun for Mei and Jason when their two year old toddlers could run at fifty KPH, or for Ellette and Justin with their Elvettes, as they called their twins, were flying round the room even before they could walk.

Eventually everything settled down, the world followed the Elves guidance, and everybody lived happily ever after.

Well, what did you expect, after all. It is a Fairy story.

The end

(possibly)

PART 5

THE NEXT GENERATION

Scotland: the land of the Unicorn, and we have our fair share of Dragons as well.

Dragons, what Dragons?

Just what do you believe?

Normal baby sitters just could not cope with Ellette's flying two year old twin girls or Mie's two year old boy toddler twins that could run at fifty kilometres per hour, so Snowball and Rainbow, with help from the girls husbands, made great baby sitters, well what child would not want to be looked after by a two and a half metre tall fluffy white Gorilla and a purring Rainbow coloured tiger, giving Ellette and Mei time to chill out, and have a chat.

Although Mei was now twenty five years old, married to Jason, and a mum, she was still young at heart, Ellette was married to Justin, Jason's cousin.

After the excitement of the last few years had died down and everybody had gone back to their normal, or in some cases not so normal lives, Ellette noticed that Mei was looking a bit troubled.

"Come on Mei out with it what is bothering you?"

"Well, Ellette there is something I have been meaning to ask you, there is one Magical creature that has never been talked about."

"What creature is that?"

"What **we** both are."

"I Know both of us are Magical."

"Yes, I know we are, but we are also Dragons."

"Are you calling us and women in general, Dragons?"

"No. we were both born in the Chinese year of the Dragon."

"Oh, I see so what you are saying, what do you want to know?"

"Dragons, is there, or was there such things as fire breathing people eating dragons?" Mei asked.

"I was told by the High Elves never to mention or talk about Dragons" Ellette explained.

"Why not, what's wrong with Dragons, most countries in the world have Dragon legends, in China stories go back hundreds of years, or in some cases thousands of years. Are they real or not?"

Ellette sat quietly for a short time trying to decide what to say to Mei. Being an Elf Queen comes with great responsibility. She finally made up her mind to tell her. After all, she was the queen, so nobody could tell her she should or shouldn't do.

"Yes Mei, Dragons are real."

"Did you just say Dragons are real" as predictable, Mei's voice rose in pitch and eyes went wide "you mean there are still Dragons in the world today" Ellette nodded "so, where are they?"

"Hiding, always hiding."

"WHERE?" Mei exclaimed. "Where are they?"

"Where nobody would look for them."

"People had searched for them, and other magical creatures for hundreds of years, but never found them, until you come along, are Dragons so Magical?"

"Dragons are not magical, but they are mythical, they are very special in their own way, normally they do not exist in our world, but they can be brought into our world."

"If they don't exist in our world then where do they exist? And why have people been making up stories about them for such a long time?"

"Dreams, Dragons are brought to life and live in peoples dream world."

"But dreams aren't real."

"Mei, how many times have you told me that what you dreamed about felt so real?" Ellette continued "I started dreaming about Lightning, Hairy Knees, and the others and I made them real."

"So, you are telling me that some people can make their dreams become real, like yourself. and if they dream about Dragon's they can become real as well?"

"Basically, YES, some dreams can come true."

"I guess there are not that many people who can do that? Can you do it?" Mei was getting excited all over again.

"Me, No. Elves cannot do it, and I am now Elvish, and remember I was given the Fairy gift of magic so that I could bring my magical helpers to life. Only a few special people have been able to do it."

"AW, what a shame. But you are saying, if the right person, or the wrong person dreamt about a fire breathing Dragon, then one could have existed in this world, or could exist in this world right now."

"Yes, can you imagine what would happen if people thought that a fire breathing Dragon was loose in the world."

"Ellette, are you trying to tell me that there is a fire breathing Dragon loose in the world?"

"Fire breathing, No, non-fire breathing, yes."

"A huge real live, scaly, bat winged. sharp taloned, arrow tailed green Dragon is alive right now, how do you know this?"

"It was recorded in the ancient Elvish book, that many thousands of years ago a group of Elves actually met a Dragon and learned all they could about them."

"Where, where did they meet it, him, her or whatever it was?" Mei's excitement was showing again.

"In a nearby country"

"Do you know where?" Mei's excitement was now overflowing.

"I don't know exactly where, but I do now of something who could find our elusive Dragon."

"But if Dragons are not Magical how could a huge green Dragon stay hidden for such a long time?"

"The Elvish book says nothing about the size or the colour of the Dragon. It just says that it was friendly and very shiny."

"Can we go and try to find it, if it still living, maybe it was the one that Saint George killed?" Mei sounded a bit deflated.

"I have read all about that, most people say that story was not true, it was just made up."

"So, what are we going to do?"

"We could go Dragon hunting, and use Lightning as our guide, he can help us find the Dragon."

"So, where do we start looking?"

"Well, the nearest country that still uses a Dragon as part of their heritage is Wales, so we go there, are you ready to go now, there's no time like the present, the boys with the help of Snowball and Rainbow can look after the kids for a few days" Ellette told Mie.

"That will be quite a challenge for them, but I'm sure they will manage, and we can go and have another adventure."

Predictable as ever Mie screamed with excitement.

Travelling to Wales would not a problem, Ellette would fly, she was the Elf Queen and had beautiful wings of her own, and Mei, although she could run very fast she could not compete with the speed of Lightning, so she would ride on Lightning's back, when there, they would find one of the Welsh Elvish communities and stay with them, hopefully they would be given more information about the history and the possible whereabouts of the elusive Dragon.

Journeys can be challenging or they can be fun. Although the distance they had to travel was about two hundred and fifty Kilometres they arrived quite quickly, as they did not have to follow the roads, Lightning could run over water, and galloping over hills and mountains would just added to Mei's excitement. Before they left their home in the Scottish borders, and heading through the nearby forest, Mei noticed that Lightning was looking very seriously at Ellette, then looked over at her, although he could not speak, he was good at making his thoughts understood.

"Ellette, I think Lightning is trying to tell us something."

Lightning has nodding his head in confirmation of Mei's observation.

"Lightning?" Ellette asked him "Do you want a challenge? do you want a race?"

Lightning nodded so much harder.

Mei put on her back pack mounted lightning, then set off as fast as they could. Ellette had to work very hard to keep pace with Lightning because he was so fast. On most of the journey Mei screamed with joy with Ellette flying overhead, laughing at Mei's antics.

When they reached the Solway Firth, part of the border Between Scotland and England, Lightning just kept running as fast as he could. At this point the estuary was not very wide, and they soon crossed over into Cumbria where they tried to avoid towns and cities, running instead over the countryside. Soon they were approaching the Lake district, which was full of rugged Mountains and beautiful Lakes. Even these obstacles did not slow Lightning down, he powered up steep hills and mountain sides, leaping high into the air as he reached the top of some of the steeper mountains. Mei felt as though she was flying. Lighting jumped over trees, roads and rivers, as if they were not there. As they approached Lake Windermere, Mei leaned forward and asked Lighting 'can you do it?' Lightning lifted his head and neighed loudly, then thundered past Ambleside and headed straight for the end of the Lake which is eighteen kilometres long. Lightning sprang into the air and landed on the Lake's surface with a loud splash, then he just kept running on the surface of the Lake, causing spray to rise to a great height in his wake. Bright sunshine caused rainbows to form and dance within the spray which followed the galloping Unicorn. Mei sat up straight and spread her arms as wide as she could, as if she was standing in the prow of a fast moving boat. Journey's should always be treated as an adventure.

They crossed over the border into Wales, then headed towards the tree covered Snowdonia National park where they quickly found an Elvish Community in a clearing among they numerous trees, Elves like to live among the trees.

"We win" Mei shouted as they landed.

"I was holding back to let you win" Ellette told her.

They both had a good laugh, winning was not required, having fun was much more important.

As they were discussing the journey an Elf lord appeared and escorted them into the meeting hall where they met with the High Elf. He had been told of Ellette's arrival, he gathered the senior elves of the community, quickly dressed in his finest golden robes and smoothed out his long silver hair. It was an odd meeting because the High Elf was dressed to meet his Queen, and she was wearing jeans and trainers, Mei was wearing a T-shirt and Ellette had on a casual Halter top instead of a T-shirt. It was an odd meeting because he expected Ellette to be dressed as a Queen should, in all her Queenly finery, but he carried out his duties with dignity, even although he did look and sound a bit embarrassed.

"How can I be of assistance my Queen?"

"We are trying to find out more about the history of the Welsh Dragon, and try to find one if possible, what information can you give us?"

"We do not discuss that history" The high Elf looked shocked that Ellette would even ask about it.

"Why?" Ellette asked.

"I was one of the group of elves that encountered the Dragon all those thousands of years ago, and we promised that we would never reveal any information about it to anybody else. How did you find out about the Dragon?"

"I read about it in the ancient book that was in the library of the hotel attached to an Elvish community where I was born."

"That information should never have been written down" The high Elf stated angrily.

"Why is it so important this information is not spoken about?"

"There is, and has always been, only one Dragon in this world, all Dragon history started in this country, can you imagine what would happen if that information was released to the human world that a Dragon was still living, they would tear everything apart looking for it"

"Is he, she or it, still living?"

"We do not know, but as far as we do know, there is nothing in this world that can kill a Dragon."

"Not even St George?" Mei asked.

"Especially not St George" they laughed "But I cannot give you any information about where it could be, even if it is still in this country."

"Is it a huge fire breathing Dragon?" Me asked the high elf.

"I can give you no further information about the Dragon, if you want out find out more then you will have to find the Dragon yourselves."

"No problem, I have something that can find it, if it is still here."

"What can possibly find a Dragon who does not want to be found?" the High Elf asked.

"Lightning" Ellette called, Lightning appeared "The most Magical creature ever to exist, if anything can find the Dragon Lightning can, we thank you for the kindness you have shown us, we do not want to impose further on your hospitality but with your permission we would like to stay in your community till Lightning has carried out his search for the Dragon"

"We would be delighted to have you as our guests for as long as you wish" He then bowed.

Wales is not a big country, but when you are looking for a needle in a haystack, the haystack does not need to be big to cause you problems.

Ellette let Lightning run free and travel wherever he wished, he searched all the magical places and met with many magical creatures trying to gather information on the location of the dragon. Finally, after four days of searching Lightning returned, full of excitement, even more excited than Mei was. They left as soon as they could. Mie got on his back and Lightning led them to the north west of the country, to one of the largest Castles in the area, Caernarfon Castle on the banks of the river, Afton Seiont, where it joined the Menai Straight. Caernarfon castle was built in the thirteenth century, and it was huge, they landed on the grass in the centre of the of the walled enclosure.

"What are we looking for Ellette?" Mei asked.

"A Dragon of course."

"Yes, I know that, but how will we find it, this is a really big castle with lots of places to hide."

"Lightning, lead us to the Dragon" He shank down to the same size of a medium sized dog so that he could lead them through what seemed like kilometres of long winding and sometimes very narrow passages of the castle, up steep staircases, and down steep slopes many of which were very dark, because often there was no windows. They followed very closely. All of a sudden, he stopped and looked into a narrow crack in a wall. The crack was only about ten centimetres wide.

"There can't be a Dragon in there, it's too small, all the stories about Dragons describe them as being big and powerful" Mei commented.

"Remember most of the people who tell stories do exaggerate somewhat, the truth does tend to get stretched". They both bent down to look into the narrow crack. Two small bright red eyes looked back out at them.

"I am Ellette, Queen of all Magical and Mythical creatures, please come out so that we can see you."

The eyes flashed once then they started to move closer.

What emerged from the crack was a gold coloured thirty centimetre long perfectly formed miniature Dragon, complete with wings and arrow shaped tail, and not breathing fire. He flew out and landed on the top of Lightning's head and wrapped his tail as best he could, round Lightnings crystal horn.

"He's so small and so cute" Mei said "No wonder nobody could find him, I think a lot of these so called brave people that said they fought Dragons were all telling whoppers of lies. What did the book say about him?"

"It just said that he would be very difficult to find, and at that size I am not surprised."

"Just imagine what people would do to him if they found him."

"I can fix that. I bestow on you the Fairy gift of invisibility."

"But we can still see him."

"Only those who are Magical or Mythical can see him, the rest of the human race cannot. He will be safer now, and we can let the others know of his existence without putting him in any danger" The small dragon lowered his head as if to say thank you.

"Wait, I have a better idea, he must be so lonely, living on his own all these thousands of years. He can come home with me" she smiled "I can't wait to see my mums face when I tell her I now have a pet Dragon."

The End of this part of the story

PART 6

THE MAGICAL SCHOOL DAYS OF THE TWIN TWINS

For the teachers and other pupils, it would prove to be a quite a challenge.

*Y*ou are five years old, can you imagine going to school on your first day and finding that two of your new friends and class mates, twin girls, have wings and can fly, and another two, twin boys can run at fifty kilometres per hour, that would be magic wouldn't it. Then you find out that the girls are the twin daughters of Fairy Queen Ellette, and the boys are the twin sons of her friend Mei, who is a very special Elf friend, and even better, or worse, that each set of twins is identical.

Ellette and Mei had married cousins whose dads were twins, so the children's granddads on their dad's side of the family were identical twins, so they all have the same surname, McKay, this could get very confusing.

Some of the pupils knew them already because they lived quite close to the twin's home. Many of the new pupils got to know each other when they went to nursery school, but the twins never went to nursery, Ellette and Mei thought that it would be unfair on the teachers to deal with the four magical children, they tended to be quite mischievous, and like so many five year olds they had so much energy.

Because the twins were more unusual than other children their parents decided on unusual names for them.

After the class has settled into their new classroom it was time for them to learn about their teacher and classmates.

"Good Morning. My name is Miss Cameron, and I will be your teacher this year. Now it seems that we have some very special children with us, Scarlet and Tilly, and Max and Gabriel, would you stand up please."

The four of them stood up looking very embarrassed, they did not like to be the centre of attention, well, unless they wanted to be.

Gabriel raised his hand.

"Yes Gabriel, what would you like to tell us?"

"Please Miss, we are not more special than anybody else, our parents say we are just more different."

"My, you are a very confident young man" Miss Cameron told him.

"Everyone has a different talent Miss Cameron" Max smiled then added "ours are just a bit different than others. But our mums made us promise not to use magic in school".

There was a Chorus of calls from many of the other pupils all saying a similar thing "Show us some magic."

"Children, calm down please, they have already promised their parents that they would not do any magic in school" then she added to herself 'Hopefully.'

A couple of weeks into their first term, Friday afternoon and Scarlet and Tilly arrived home from school, they were full of excitement.

They had been picked up and brought home by Mei who's turn it was to do the school run.

"Mum, mum, mum, mum, mum. mum" they shouted as they entered the house.

"Calm down you two sound like a machine gun."

"Mum, it's show and tell on Monday morning at school and Miss Cameron says we can take our pets to school as long as a parent is there to take them home when we're finished." Tilly shouted full of excitement.

"Can we take Hairy Knees with us to show the rest of the class?" Scarlett added.

"Please mum, can we, can we take Hairy Knees?" Tilly was almost crying with excitement.

"I don't think a huge blue Tarantula spider would be allowed in the classroom, I'm sure a few of your classmates would get very frightened." Ellette told them. "Remember she is so much bigger than you are. How about taking Henrietta to show them she is a more normal size?"

The girls looked so disappointed; they hung their heads in frustration.

"Oh mum." Scarlet said sadly.

"But we need something that is really special, something that nobody else has." Tilly said sadly.

"I am sure that nobody else has a Red kneed tarantula." Ellette said quietly, trying to calm them down, and failing.

"I don't suppose we could take our Gold Dragon then?" Tilly asked shyly.

"You already know the answer to that question, no you can't."

"Ok, well there is one more thing that we thought we could take mum." the girls looked at each other.

"I get the feeling that I am not going to like this. Come on then what is it?" Ellette asked.

"Well, we could take **you**, nobody else has a Queen as a parent, and you could go in your full Queeny outfit."

"Please mum, please?" Tilly pleaded.

Ellette thought to herself, what five year old would not want to show off her mum to the rest of her class. Some of the others in the class knew who she was, or they had seen pictures of her, but few of them had seen her in her Queenly robes.

"Ok, I give in to your logic. Now, I wonder what the boys next door are going to do for their show and tell? I need to call Mei."

"We don't know what they will do, but ours will be the best show and tell ever." Scarlet said proudly.

Show and tell time.

This was not a typical Monday morning, the school entrance and playground was so much busier than usual, not only parents with their children, but so many of them were holding puppies, kittens. and other small furry animals as well as boxes and bags of things to show their classmates. Max and Gabriel were throwing a tennis ball to each other and scarlet and Tilly were standing beside their mums talking quietly to each other. All the parents knew who Ellette and Mei were, but some were looking sideways at them trying to figure out what their children were going to show the rest of the class.

The doors opened and the children ran excitedly to their classroom, followed by their proud parents who were allowed to stand at the back of the classroom, ready to help out if any of the small animals escaped.

Boxes were opened, bags were emptied, puppies and kittens were cuddled, and excitement and wonder filled the classroom. Miss Cameron was a new teacher, so she was being monitored by her head teacher who was standing at the back of the classroom talking to the parents.

"Right children who is going to be first? Let's start at the front lefthand side of the front row and then move backwards each row at a time."

Children brought forward boxes and bags of toys or things they had made, or a special fluffy or hairy friend. All presentations were met with OO's, Ah's, cheers, and enthusiastic applause.

Then it was the girls turn.

"Can we go last please Miss Cameron." Scarlet asked politely.

"If you wish. Right Max and Gabriel, it's your turn."

The boys walked to the front of the class and then they walked to opposite sides of the room, each of them was carrying a tennis ball.

"We would like to show you our special skill." they through the balls across the room to each other, catching them easily.

"Careful you don't hit anybody else please." Miss Cameron could see that the head teacher was looking a bit concerned.

"We'll be careful, time to speed up a bit" Max told Gabriel. They not only started to throw the balls faster, they started to throw them further away from each other, then run faster to catch them, they were like a blur moving back and forward to catch the balls. The other children started to cheer and encourage them to go faster.

"You have shown us enough of your talent, I think you should stop now." Miss Cameron called. The boys stopped, and they weren't even out of breath. The whole class cheering and clapping, they had never seen anybody that could run that fast, especial not a five year old.

"Your turn now Tilly and Scarlet." Miss Cameron said quietly trying, and failing, to calm the class down. Tilly and Scarlet walked to the front on the class, turned, smiled then said together.

"What we have to show you today is our mum, mum please come and join us." Ellette started to walk towards the front of the class. It was only at this point that the others noticed that Ellette was still wearing a long dark blue cloak with a hood, the hood was up and was covering her head to just above her eyes. She stopped, then turned, with a twin on either side of her.

"Everybody here knows who our mum is, but not many will have seen her as she really is, as the Fairy Queen Elf."

Ellette untied the cord at the neck of her cloak, of the hood back from her hair and let the cloak fall to the floor behind her, then spread her wings.

Everybody in the room gasped.

"Wow, look at all the Diamonds." one of the children said.

"What a beautiful dress." Another added.

"She's just like a Fairy Queen." one of the boys commented.

"She is a Fairy Queen." a girl told him "Boys" she sighed.

"That is a lot of diamonds." One of the parents stated.

"Must have cost a fortune" another of the patents commented.

The high necked deep red full length dress had long sleeves and a small raised collar, the whole dress sparkled in the sunshine as if it was covered in diamonds. Her long blonde hair was tied back, and a very fine crystal Tiara Hamsa rested on her forehead.

"These are not diamonds." Ellette informed them. "Elves have no use for useless or impractical things, what you see is Quartz Crystal and glass and very fine silver thread. I made the dress myself. Elves are a very practical race. We do not take wantonly from earth's resources, but we do like pretty things."

"But we thought that you weren't an Elf?" someone asked.

"I was not born an Elf, but at birth I was given the wisdom of the elves, and the magic of the Fairy's." Ellette told them.

"Can you do magic?" one of the boys asked.

"Yes I can." Ellette told him.

"What's the best magic you can do?" Another pupil asked.

Ellette sighed, 'I knew this would happen' the said to herself then she whispered 'Lightning' so as not to alarm the children too much, a small fluffy silver Unicorn appeared between the rows of seats, then he started to grow, soon her horse sized magnificent Silver Unicorn was standing there between the rows of children.

The children's screams of excitement were heard all over the school. Even the parents gasped, and some screamed as the sight of a Unicorn in school.

That show and tell event was going to be talked about for a long, long time.

"I think we need to do something to calm the children down." Ellette said to Miss Cameron.

"If you could do that It really would be magical." Miss Cameron replied.

Ellette spoke quietly to Tilly and Scarlet who took off their jackets, unfurled their wings then flew round the room sprinkling Fairy dust on all the children, and the parents, who were starting to look a bit anxious about what was happening.

"This is just Fairy dust. it will make them relax and it will wear off before the end of the day." Ellette told Miss Cameron, then she blew some in her direction. Miss Cameron took a deep breath, smiled, then she as well started to relax.

"I think it is time for parents to gather up their pets and head home and let the school get back to normal." Queen Ellette was now in charge.

Over the next few months things quietened down at home. Surprisingly, enthusiasm for schoolwork and school activities kept the four children busy, well not really that busy, but busy enough to keep them from getting up to too much mischief.

Ellette's little angels

Friday afternoon was normally the day when new things started to happen. The door burst open as usual, and the two girls came running into the room, they were not allowed to fly inside the house.

"Mum, mum we're little angels" they shouted together, as they often did, just one of these things that twins often do.

"Calm down, I know I often call you my little monsters, but calling you angels is going a bit too far."

"Nooooo, it's Christmas soon and we are to be angels, and we are to fly above the school nativity play."

Now this was something new, Ellette thought to herself.

"I'm delighted for you both, but what about the boys?" Ellette asked.

"Oh, they are not happy, cos they're only to be shepherds."

"Shepherds are a very important part of the story" Ellette told them.

"But they wanted to be wise men." Tilly replied.

"Well, you can't be the best or fastest at everything."

Christmas was approaching fast, and it was a Friday afternoon yet again.

"Mum mum, the teacher wants you to come to the school." The twins shouted,

"What have you done wrong that she wants to see me at school?" Ellette asked.

"Mum, we've done nothing wrong, she wants all the parents to be there for the dress rehearsal for the nativity play." Ellette was informed by Scarlet.

Tilly took a deep breath. "The dress rehearsal is to be held the day before the nativity, in the school hall some days before the school stops for the Christmas holiday. She wants the parents of the children taking part to come along to the dress rehearsal, to help out with costumes and also supervise their little monsters, eh, I mean little performers,

I'm just so smart." Tilly giggled.

Dress Rehearsal Time

"Right children, line up in the order I put you in so that the proper characters go in first, where are my wise men and shepherds" Max and Gabriel were looking very guilty "there you are, good, don't you all look so smart. Ok choir in you go and take up your positions" Trying to organise twenty four young performers is never an easy task, even with lots of parent helpers.

"Music please." Miss Cameron called. The music teacher started to play a Christmas carol then the choir started to sing.

"Mary and Joseph, in you go and take up your positions, angels, off you go and fly over them, now shepherds it's your turn."

Max and Gabriel stepped forward, both were carrying what seemed like toy sheep, until one of them jumped down and started to run away, it looked like a short legged long tailed cotton wool covered golden footed sheep.

"What is happening here?" Cried Miss Cameron.

"We'll get it." Gabriel told her, and he and Max started to run after the escaping sheep, the boys were laughing so hard, and so were the flying angels, and so were the rest of the children.

Mei whispered to Ellette. "That looks very much like a small dragon dressed up as a sheep." Ellette nodded in agreement. "Just wait till I get those boys home." Mei added.

The boys finally caught the sheep, well dragon sheep, and ran back into the dressing room, straight into their mum and Ellette.

"Well explain yourselves." Mei said angrily.

"Aw mum, we were just having a bit of fun, and so was the dragon." Max said smiling.

"I don't think Miss Cameron found it very funny, and the dragon was to be kept secret, luckily nobody else knew it was a dragon dressed up as a sheep." Ellette told them.

"Aw, aunty Ellette, will we be punished?"

"Oh yes, you will be punished, just not sure how yet, but your mum and I will make it suitable."

"Now go and apologise to Miss Cameron." their mum told them.

The boys hung their heads and walked slowly through to tell Miss Cameron. After they left Mei and Ellette looked sternly at each other then burst out laughing.

"We really shouldn't laugh, but that really was a funny prank, our children really do take after us, life is too short not to have a laugh."

Miss Cameron was shaken but saw the funny side and allowed the boys to still be shepherds as long as they did not pull any other pranks during the real nativity. Like the show and tell, it really was a performance to be remembered, well what other school can say they had real flying angels at their nativity.

Miss Cameron was often heard saying to herself. "what's going to happen next?" then she would shake her head, smile then carry on.

You call that music.

Most young children like music, and the first year at school is often the best time to get them started and find out what instrument suites their ability and personality. The double twins, at first, were so keen to try different instruments, but the boy's speed at doing things ruled out most stringed instruments, they could not stand up to the punishment. Their next favourite was the drums but the noise they made was just, well too noisy.

"But mum, we like playing the drums, the noise can't be that bad, can it?" Max pleaded.

"We had complaints from our neighbours three doors away, and we all live in detached houses. So no, no drums, and that is my last word about drums." Mei was determined that they would not be playing any drums. "But I have spoken to your music teacher, and he says that you would both be very welcome to learn to play the triangle."

"Muuuum, you are kidding, you can't make us play the triangle?" Gabriel was very upset, Mei just smiled.

"Mum you are so weird sometimes" Max stated. Mei just kept smiling.

The girls, being the little angels they were, well thought they were, wanted to learn to play the harp.

"But mum, that's what angels play, and well you just pluck the strings and music is done, we have tried the violin, and they don't play very well, and the cellos are just so big and difficult to play." Scarlet stated.

"Scarlet, do they have any harps at school for you to practice on." Ellette asked.

"No, but you can buy us harps, then we can take **them** to school." Scarlet said smiling.

"Now listen, there are two problems with that, one, harps are big and very heavy, and two, they cost a lot of money."

"You can buy us smaller harps, cos they will cost less." Tilly stated then smiled.

"That type of harp is out if the question. I have spoken to your music teacher, and she has suggested an instrument that is like a harp, and you use keys to make the sound instead of plucking the strings." Ellette told them.

"Never heard of a harp like that." Scarlet said looking and sounding confused.

"Oh, I think you have, it's called a piano."

"And the boys call Aunt Mei weird." they said together.

For the four young musicians, music practice plinked and plonked and tinkled on.

Magic time

Friday afternoon, springtime and the sun was shining on the school garden, shoots were springing up, insects were flying about, and crawling over the young plants, and young birds were feeding on the insects. It was the first year's turn to spend time in the garden. They were being helped by some of the year seven children and supervised by Miss Cameron. They all heard a soft thud. A small bird had just flown into the window of the garden shed.

Scarlet immediately ran over to see how it was.

"Miss, it's hurt its wing."

"Poor little thing." Tilly said as she joined her sister.

Scarlet was holding the bird in her cupped hands.

"I'll get rid of it for you miss." One of the older boys said as her reached for the bird.

"NO" Scarlet screamed at him then pulled the bird closer to her chest. The twins looked at each other and nodded their heads.

"We can help it get better." Tilly told Miss Cameron.

"Remember your parents said no magic in school." she informed them.

"This isn't just magic its caring for others that are hurt, you would want us to help if one of the other children was hurt, so we're going to help this little bird, because we are more fairies and elves than human, and that's what Elves do." Tilly cupped her hands over Scarlets, then they both said 'HEAL'

After a few seconds they felt the bird flutter in their hands, they open their hands and the bird flew up and landed on Scarlets head, whistled a beautiful tune as if to say thank you, then it flew away.

This Friday afternoon the house door opened, and the girls entered very quietly.

"Miss Cameron phoned me, so I know all about the little bird and what happened at school." Ellette stood there looking very cross.

"I know we are not allowed to do magic at school, but we had to heal the little bird, it deserved to have a chance in life, it wasn't the birds fault somebody put the shed in its way." Scarlet pleaded.

"I'm very proud of both of you for doing the right thing. You are too young to understand yet, but some day you will learn that sometimes doing what you have been told is wrong, is actually the right thing to do." then she gave them both a huge hug.

The next challenge

Sports day was getting close. Just how do normal children compete when racing against girls that can fly or boys that can run superfast. Miss Cameron had the idea of asking their mums for help and see if anything could be done.

"Well." Ellette told her "I could bind, I mean switch off their powers, for a short time, but I don't think they will be very pleased about it, they do like to use their special abilities."

"I have an idea about a challenge we can use to compensate for them becoming more normal." Miss Cameron told them what her idea was.

"Now, that is a challenge I feel would satisfy them, at least for a short time, please let us know how it goes" Mei laughed.

Gym time was never a happy time for most of the other children.

"Miss Cameron, what is the point of playing games the twins always win anyway." She was often told.

"I have spoken to the twins parents, and they have agreed that on the sport day, the twins have already been told that they will not have their normal extra powers." The twins did not look very happy. "But until that happens, I have a new challenge for them."

"What is it Miss?" someone asked.

"We are going to play a new game, Dodge type football, but with a difference. Everybody go and get a tennis racket and a tennis ball, not Max and Gabriel, wait there please, Tilly and Scarlet you can go and get a racket and ball, this is going to be the rest of the class against you four."

"Twenty against four?" max said thoughtfully "That should be about right."

"Max, Tilly, Gabriel, and Scarlet you will guard the wall at that end of the Gym, the rest of you will try to hit the wall with a tennis ball. Now, this is not a competition, it's not about winning or losing, it's about finding out if something can be done, right class line up long the middle of the gym, ready? GO."

Twenty tennis rackets connected with twenty balls which flew towards the twins end of the gym hall. Stopping twenty balls at one time was a real challenge for the twins, but stopped they were, and were hit back by Scarlet and tilly, or they were thrown or kicked back towards the waiting rackets again by Max and Gabriel, only to be hit back towards them again. Balls were flying all over the place, some high and some low, back and forwards as fast as they could be returned, and the squeals of fun and delight were getting louder. The smallest girl in the class, her name was Jenni, but was often called Lil' Jen, she was even smaller than Tilly and Scarlet who were really small, just like their mum. Jenni was keeping well out of the way of the melee, she was staying close to one of the side walls, a ball landed at her feet and an idea flashed through her mind, she slowly and quietly bent down and picked up the ball, then she started to make her way slowly along the wall towards the other end of the gym hall, nobody was taking any notice of her. When she was about two metres from the wall she stepped out and threw the ball at the wall. The twins were so busy they did not see her until it was too late, the ball hit the wall, and Jenni screamed at the top of her voice **"I did it, I did it, I did it."**

Everybody stopped playing, and the gym went very quiet.

"Hey, what just happened?" Max shouted.

At five or six years of age achieving something is a big thing to do, and excitement often takes over.

"I did it, I hit the wall." Jenni screamed. Then she picked up the ball and through it at the wall again, then everybody started to scream at once.

Max and Gabriel ran over, picked up Jenni, put her on their shoulders then ran around the gym, like in a lap of honour, she was squealing with delight.

Miss Cameron was horrified, as she was trying to get the children to quiet down the door opened and the head teacher entered the Gym.

"My this looks like they are having fun, be careful please." she said loudly.

Max and Gabriel slowed down and dropped Jenni in front of the teachers.

"That was so much fun Miss, I felt so safe with the boys carrying me." Jenni said with a huge smile.

The twin girls flew up as stood beside Jenni.

"Please Miss we all enjoyed that so much, we have a new name for that game, we should call it **Jenni's** game."

So, for the rest of their school time the game was called Jenni's game, and it was played frequently and with so much enthusiasm.

"They never told us situations like this would be part of our teaching experience." Miss Cameron whispered to the head teacher.

"Children learn by doing, not just by being taught, not all classes have magical children in them." she replied. "Children challenge teachers every day, you are doing really well, keep it up."

"At least we now have an outlet for the twins energy as a distraction during the Sports day, and the others can have an equal chance of doing well, so everybody should be happy."

Things did not go as planned on sports day, the twin boys were built like their dad, they were the biggest boys in the class, so they had the strength and the speed, even without their special talents, to run fast enough to win their races.

Sometimes you don't need extra talents for you to achieve who you are.

Challenges at school, and in life, change all the time and we need to learn who we are, and how we can deal with these growing challenges, and challenges when they went to the high school require a more confident and determined approach.

PART 7

SCORZIST MOGG

Want or need help, ask for it.

It was the day after the children's sixth birthday party.

"MUUUM" Four children's excited voices called in unison.

'I know that call' Ellette thought to herself 'somebody wants something.' Mie and Ellette were having a cuppa and a well-earned quiet chat.

Ellette's twin girls Tilly and Scarlet, and Mie's twin boys Max (Maximillian) and Gabriel had played together since the girls could fly, unlike Ellette the girls were born with wings, and the boys at about two years old, taking after their mum who had been given the Fairy gift of speed, could run at fifty kph (kilometres per hour). Mie's boys were six days older that Ellette's girls. Ellette and Mie had married cousins, who looked like twins, but were actually sons of twins, the two new sets of twins were somehow able to act and think of the same thing at the same time.

"MUUUUM the dragon's doing it again, he's getting bigger again." Gabriel called, he was the bossy one and normally took control of tricky situations.

"Your turn." Ellette said to Mie.

"Why me?" she exclaimed.

"Well, it is your son who is asking the question."

The Dragon Gabriel was talking about, who had been found for the first time over ten thousand years ago, had been a part of both their families for about four years, after he was found and brought home by Ellette and Mie. He, they always thought of him as a he, but they really were not sure if it was a male or female, but he/she or it acted like a male, He was brought home by Ellette and Mie when the children were two years old, at that time he was about thirty centimetres long, and since then he had shown no sign of growing, until recently.

"MUUUM come quickly" Gabriel shouted as he came running at full speed through from the playroom, he was quickly followed by Tilly who was flying at full speed.

"Gabriel, how often do you need to be told, no running in the house" Mie scolded.

"And Tilly, no flying in the house." Ellette added.

"Sorry mum." Replied both.

Gabriel grabbed Mie by the hand and pulled her towards the playroom.

Mie was rushed through to the playroom to find the children looking down at a forty centimetre long golden dragon.

"Too slow as usual" commented Max, who then sighed as only a six year old boy can.

"What length did he grow to." Mie asked.

Tilly held her hands wide. "About that long." Tilly and Scarlet said together.

"About one metre then." Mie said.

"We have been thinking, and we don't think he wants adults as see him as he could be."

"I wonder why?" Mie said as she bent down, picked him up, and scratched him under the chin just the same as you would do with a pet dog, he seemed to like that, he stretched his head forward for more attention.

"Did he make any noises?" she asked.

"He just sort of screeched once as if he was trying to speak, then he was quiet again, then shrank again to the size he is now, a little longer than he was before" Tilly told Mie.

Some of their mum's confidence, and Elven wisdom given to their mums seemed to have been passed on to all four of them, even at their young age of only six years old.

"Has he been getting enough to eat?" Mie asked.

"Well mum, do you ever see any flies in the house? And he does go out on his own sometimes, everything else we try giving him he just ignores, even dog or cat food" Max said he was the quiet thoughtful one.

"When was the last time you saw him grow?" Mie asked.

"When we had our birthday party last year, but we don't know why he got bigger then either" Max told her.

"I so wish he could talk so we could ask how to help him" Mie told the children.

"Maybe as our powers grow, WE will find the answer" Max stated with confidence.

"He has lived for over ten thousand years, do you know how long ten thousand years is?" Mie asked them.

"Not really, but we do know it's a long, long time. We know we are only six years old, and we know it's a lot longer than six years."

"Well, nobody has been able to help him for a long, long time, what makes you four think that you can help him."

"Because we know more about Magic that anybody else, we were born Magical, and we are smarter than most people" Max said. "so if anybody can help him, we can."

The Dragon since their sixth birthday had carried on growing about ten centimetres each year and grew just after the children's birthday party.

The time was fast approaching that their parents were dreading, their children's thirteenth birthday was approaching, and the Dragon was now one hundred and ten centimetres long. Can you just imagine trying to control four thirteen year old magical cousins? Their Magical powers and abilities were growing so quickly that their parents had a very hard time keeping up with them, both physically and intellectually. Smart precocious (annoying) children are very difficult to predict and these four were no different than other so called normal children.

Special age, so a special birthday is required. There was no Magical school for them to go to, so normal school with normal school friends who knew all about their magical background. One of the main beliefs of Eleven culture is fairness, there was no bullying at their school, because bullies would have had to face dealing with Snowball or Rainbow who often went to school with the two twins, hairy knees was not allowed to go to the school, just to look after them, it was found that having a bright blue two meter long Tarantula spider in class was a bit off putting for many pupils, and Snowball and Rainbow were friends with everyone.

It was to be a large party in Ellette's house with all their friends invited, and guess what, it was to be a Magical themed party, so many Harry Potter's and witches and wizards were expected. So, lots of people means a very large Birthday cake, no a massive birthday cake sixty centimetres square with lots of icing.

The fact that a Dragon was in the house had been kept secret, he was to be kept upstairs out of the way until all then party goers had returned home. The party was to be held on the Friday night after their actual birthday. The cake was ordered in plenty of time, just to make sure it would be delivered on time, and it was delivered on the day of the party. The teenagers were at school, Ellette and Mie stayed in that Friday morning to finish decorating the house ready for the party, so they were there when the cake was delivered. The delivery men carried it through to the table on the main dining room, it was splendid, it was covered in magical designs made out of multi coloured icing. Ellette and Mie then went out shopping returning at the same time as the four new teenagers who were bursting with excitement.

"WE WANT TO SEE THE CAKE" they shouted excitedly as they burst through the door then ran and flew into the house and through to the dining room.

Total shock, the table where the cake should have been, was covered in crumbs and the cake was missing.

"WHAT" they all shouted together "MUM, what's happened, where is the cake?"

A loud thump was heard upstairs. They scrambled through the dining room door and rushed up the stairs. Scarlet flew overhead and arrived at her bedroom door first, she burst it open and then froze.

"WOW! She screamed, look at the size of him."

Curled up on the floor was their Dragon, but not the metre or so long Dragon they had left before going to school.

They all crowded into the open door.

"Now there's something you don't see every day." Max stated quietly "He must be about eight metres long."

There were cake crumbs round his mouth and on the bedroom floor, and he looked as if he was actually smiling.

"Did you eat our cake." Tilly asked.

"Tilly, now that is just silly question, look at all the evidence." Max Added.

A Loud rumble came from the Dragons throat.

"It sounded as if he said ME." Tilly exclaimed.

"ME NEEDED CAKE, ME EAT CAKE, ME GROW." the Dragon growled.

"You can talk?" Ellette asked.

"NOT ENOUGH CAKE, NOT GROW. NOT TALK, GET CAKE AND GROW, NOW TALK." then he smiled.

"YOU CALL ME DRAGON, NOT DRAGON, ME DRAGON TYPE PERSON, ME SCORZIST MOGG."

"Is that your name Scorzist Mogg?"

"**Yes.**" Scorzist said with a smile.

"Where did you come from?" Elette asked.

He seemed to relax, and his voice mellowed, still growling softly, "Where I want to go back to, home, my home." he added sadly.

"We did not know you needed cake, we thought you needed meat, sorry. What else do you eat?" Ellette asked.

"If really hungry, eat almost anything, but prefer cake."

"Do you breathe fire?" Mie asked, they all looked at her "Well somebody had to ask." she added.

"Only when I have a very hot curry" he laughed in his throat with a very deep rumble "No, I do not breathe fire, and I do not eat people either, although I know some people get frightened when they see Scorzist"

"Other people have seen you." Mie exclaimed. "I thought that we were the first to see you since the Elves met you about ten thousand years ago."

"Do you think that I would spend all that time alone in an old damp castle when there is fun to have and a world to see. I know the human race can be silly, but I thought that you would be wiser. I wasn't always so small, cake is sometimes hard to get so I had to shrink."

"If you ate more cake, would you get even bigger than you are now?" Scarlet asked.

"No, not much, that was a big cake, this is about normal size."

"What does your name mean?"

"Scorzist Mogg means, well it can mean a lot of things, but where I come from it means...." Then he stopped.

"Come on tell us what it means please." Scarlet was getting impatient.

"In my language my name means troublemaker. So, in your language it would mean silly, crazy, obstinate, zany, idiotic, senile toad, and Mogg, that is my family name."

"You said more people had seen you, where, and how many?" Mie was getting excited again.

"Everywhere and lots of people, I was sent away from my people because Scorzist wanted to have more fun."

"You were sent away by your own people?"

"Yes, other's they say I was a troublemaker, but I only wanted to have fun, this world is fun, so many people get so excited." Scorzist explained.

"Scorzist, just where have you been in the last ten thousand years?" Ellette asked.

"Everywhere." he said excitedly, his eyes full of mirth.

"And how many people saw you?"

"So many people, me not count."

"You travelled all over the world in the last ten thousand years showing off to the people wherever you went?"

"Yes, great fun was had, but some people not like to see me, some try to hurt me, they chase me away and call me nasty names."

"No wonder there are so many stories about Dragons all over the world, people are often frightened of things they don't understand." Ellette said.

"So, all the Dragon stories are about one dragon, You?" Ellette said. The four children were listening closely.

"Yes, me so famous." Scorzist said happily.

"Infamous more like, what about the stories about you breathing fire?" Mie asked.

"Easy, me got big lungs, blow on fire, get big flames, easy."

"MUUUM, we got a problem." Tilly said.

"Yes, a big Golden one." Ellette commented.

"No, not that big one, the other big one, we have thirty party guests coming shortly, and we have no cake for them." Tilly stated calmly.

"WHAT, forgot about that." Ellette thought for a second "Boys, here's some money, run down to the shop and get more cakes, any cakes." the boys looked at her excitedly, "YES RUN, now go." so many time they had been told not to run, now they had freedom to use their gift of speed, they ran like they had never run before.

"Scorzist, no you can't go with them, you stay here." Ellette said firmly. One sulking sad dragon type person, just the same as the guests would be if they didn't get any birthday cake.

The party

Party time, Ellette opened the door in her full Queenly robes, the guests gasped at her beauty. The path leading up to the house was blocked with Wizards, Witches, Fairies and even the occasional Unicorn.

"Invitations will be collected by our door keeper, have fun" She said regally, then stepped aside to reveal Snowball standing by the door, he collected their invitations and every one of them gave him a hug, he was so well loved by everyone. Just to make sure there was no teenage tantrums Ellette had sprinkled Snowball with Fairy dust so when they cuddled him, they all got a small amount of the dust on them. They were all just so happy.

There were invisible sandwiches so you didn't know what you were eating, Dragon poo sandwiches, nobody would admit to what was in them but they tasted ok, one of the deserts was Unicorn poo, chocolate balls mixed with chocolate mouse, jellyfish jellies, goblin eyeballs and many more gruesome goodies to eat, and drink was everything from bat saliva and slug slime to muddy water.

The party had not been going for very long when the door opened and Justin and Jason arrived home from work, Justin mouthed to Ellette, 'I'll go upstairs and get changed' there was too much noise for her to hear what he said. She was about to say something in reply but they moved out before she could reply. A few seconds late she heard a loud thump from upstairs, 'oops they have landed on their backsides again'. loud footsteps were heard running down the stairs, Justin burst into the room "There's a huge Dragon in our bedroom" he shouted at Ellette.

"SHUSH" she said, nodded her head and smiled. Justin was about to say something, but he just shook his head and went back up the stairs. Unusual surprises were common in this house.

"Where is Hairy Knees." Ellette shouted "Try and find her."

Children were running about screaming with joy and excitement, "We can't find her, where is she." they called.

Ellette had made Hairy Knees invisible. She was hanging from the ceiling in the living room. All of a sudden, the two metre long bright blue Tarantula spider dropped onto the children below. The screams of joy got so much louder.

Ellette noticed on of the younger girls sitting all alone in a corner of the room. She went over and sat beside her, Rainbow was the size of an ordinary cat and had been mingling with the guests purring and rubbing herself against their legs. She came over to try and cheer the girl up.

"Hey, are you not having fun?"

"Yes, I suppose so." she replied softly, while stoking Rainbow who purred even louder.

"What's a special girl like you sitting here for?"

"I'm not special, I'm just plain ordinary me, I'm not as special as you are."

"Me, I'm not that special. We are all special in our own way, there is nobody else in the world like you, we are all different and we are all special, what is your name?"

"Julia."

"Well Julia, would you like to do something really special?"

Julia brighten up a bit. "What is it?"

"Something I did a long time ago, come with me." Ellette led her to the front door, which she opened to reveal Lightning standing in the front garden. "The first time I rode on his back I got so excited I screamed all the way home. Would you like to go for a ride?"

Wide eyed and full of newfound excitement Julia said. "YES PLEASE."

Ellette lifted her on to Lightnings back. "He won't let you fall off. Go." she called, lightning reared up and took off as fast as lightning, with Julia on his back, screaming with joy.

Ellette had had an idea about how to end the party, which was planned for midnight. She went up the stairs to make final arrangements.

Just before midnight she called all the party goers to the front door and ushered them out into the front garden.

"Up on the roof we have arranged a special silent fireworks display, we don't want to frighten the neighbours or their pets. Are you ready?"

"YE.S" they all screamed.

The fireworks started with a shower of sparks, then rockets shot up into the night sky. Up behind the sparks a huge Golden Dragon flew up and reached the rockets just as they burst open. The children screamed even louder when they saw the dragon, Ellette had already remover his gift of invisibility. They thought that it was part of the fireworks display, until it flew down and landed in the garden beside them. Just how loud would you scream?

Everyone talked about the party for months, all said it was the best party ever, EVER. But that was not the end of the party, Scorzist had agreed to fly some of the children home. He flew them to their houses, then stood behind them when they knocked on their door. When their parents opened the door, he would lean forward and go "BOO" the children were so excited to see their parents running away from the friendliest Dragon ever. Scorzist thought that this was about the greatest fun he had ever had.

"Ellette, there is an eight metre long Dragon curled up on our bed" Justin stated after all the party guests had gone home. "What are we going to do about him?"

"He ate the birthday cake and just, grew bigger."

Mie and Jason were about to take their children home, next door.

"He wants to go home." Max told them. "He loves it here, but he would also like to go back home to his family, he has been away for a very long time."

"We will talk about this later today after we have all had a good night's sleep." Ellette told them.

Mie, Jason, and the boys left to go next door, Tilly and Scarlet went to their own room.

"We still have a Dragon asleep on our bed, what are we going to do about it?" Justin asked Ellette.

"Spare room it is then for us tonight."

Justin was not pleased.

"If you are not happy about it, then go wake up Scorzist and ask him to move." Ellette smiled, then walked along to the spare room, followed by her grumpy husband.

Later that morning the two families, plus Scorzist were sitting having a late breakfast, left over party food, there was even some cake left over, which made Scorzist very happy. Although he was only half a metre wide, he did take up a lot of space. Everyone was still sleepy, so the rest of that day was spent clearing up the mess the party goers had left. The four teenagers had spent a lot of time together speaking in whispers.

"All right." Ellette said. "What is all the whispering about?"

"We want to help Scorzist get home." Gabriel took control of the situation.

"You are only thirteen years old, too young to be old and too old to be called youngsters." Ellette said.

"We are young adults, and you keep telling us we have to take some responsibility for our actions, so why not let us help Scorzy get home? We are not children anymore."

"Scorzy?" Justin asked.

"Our pet name for him, I think he likes it."

Scorzy smiled, then nodded his scaly head.

"The four of you have obviously been planning this, so where will you start?" Mie asked.

"We have already started, Scorzy has told us that Lightning is the key to him getting home, he was so excited when Lightning found him, he said it was fate." Scarlet told them.

"Scorzy says he came here through the land of the Unicorns, and through big deep water. Lightning should know where the land of the Unicorns is." Tilly added.

"Scotland is the land of the Unicorns, so somewhere in Scotland is the way back to his home" Max told them.

"Lightning." Ellette called, Lightning appeared. "How do we get to the home of the Unicorns?" Ellette asked him.

He shook his head vigorously.

"We just want to find out how to get Scorzist home, he says he came through the home of Unicorns."

Lightning looked at Scorzist who said "Please."

Lightning stood quietly for a few seconds then turned and left the house.

"He has gone to fetch something." Scorzist told them. "He may be away for a long time."

They all sat quietly for a short time.

"Scorzist, you told us you came through deep dark water?" Scarlet asked, she was the thinker of then four of them.

"Yes."

"Somewhere in Scotland?"

"Yes."

"Could that have been Lock Ness?" she asked.

"Could have been it was a long time ago."

"Did people see you there?"

"Could have done."

"Are you what they call the Lock Ness Monster?"

"Could be." he said shyly.

"I thought the Loch Ness monster was a greenish colour and huge. You're not big enough to the monster." Max said.

"Well, can sort of change colour, and size, when want to."

"Go on change colour then." Tilly requested.

"What colour you want me to be?" Scorzist asked.

"Let's start with green then."

"Ok, light green or dark green?"

"Both." Challenged Tilly.

His golden scale shimmered then turned dark green on his back and light green on his underbelly.

"Pete's Dragon." Tilly laughed.

"Now change size." She called.

Scorzist started to take in a really deep breath, he started to blow up just like a balloon, he was now over a meter wide and still growing.

"Ok, that is enough, we believe you." Ellette said.

"How many times have you been back to Loch Ness?" Gabriel took up the questioning.

"Quite few times."

"No wonder no one could not find you, you were away somewhere else. Can you live underwater?" Max asked.

"Yes, can, if have to."

"You can live with someone for years then in one day find out so much more about them." Ellette commented.

Living with flying teenagers can be challenging, but add to that an eight metre long Dragon, who only wants get up to mischief, and have fun in the house, then things can get a bit stressful. Expectations were high that Lightning would return soon with information that would help Scorzist get home.

A Week later the school holidays were approaching and Lightning had not returned. As expected, having a Dragon in the house was not going to be a secret for very long. News and TV vans were a common sight outside the house, but it was decided that to let Scorzist be seen or even talked to, would not be a good idea. On the Friday after the schools broke up for the holidays it was decided that an evening out at a fast food outlet would be a good idea, well it was to start with, the two families, four adult and four teenagers, they left Scorzist at home with enough cake to keep him happy, they were used to being stared at when they were out shopping, the people in the local area all knew who they were and accepted their presence in the community. They were sitting in the Burger house when the people around them started to get noisy and were pointing to something outside, then someone shouted 'Dragon,' and some people started to panic.

"It's all right." Ellette shouted. "We know him he's a friend of ours." The burger bar was not big enough to let Scorzist come inside so they went outside to see why he was there. Standing next to Scorzist was Lightning, he had returned home.

"Thought it would be a good idea to come and see you as soon as he got home, he has something to show you."

The crowd of people inside the Burger bar were all pressed up against the windows to see what was happening.

At that point, the Manager arrived.

"It's ok, we can explain." Ellette said to him.

"NO, all I want is a photograph, if you don't mind?"

Scorzist turned toward him. smiled and said "Cheese" then added. "life should always be this funny."

"We will allow you to take a photograph on condition that you give a free meal to any homeless person that comes to you for a meal, have we got a deal?"

The manager was not happy because it wasn't company policy give away food for free, but he agreed, because the photo would be great for publicity. Ellette and family did not normally look for publicity, but in the name of charity rules can be broken.

Scorzist stretched out to his full length with Max and Gabriel sitting on his back, the four adults stood behind him with Tilly and Scarlet hovering overhead, and Lightning standing by his tail.

"We would also like copy of our own please." Mie stated.

All the manager could say was "WOW" before walking back into his restaurant.

Tilly flew to give Lightning a hug.

"There's a small bag hanging from his mane." she untied it and took it over to her mum.

Ellette opened the bag and took out a small crystal Unicorn horn.

"**The Key.**" Scorzist called loudly.

"Is this the key." Ellette asked Lightning.

 He nodded in confirmation.

"Where did you get it?" Ellette asked.

Lightning shook his head vigorously.

"Do you know where we have to take this key?" Scarlet asked.

Lightning nodded.

"Excellent. The four of us are going on an adventure." Scarlet added excitedly.

 Mie looked disappointed. The boys went over and gave their mum a hug.

"Don't worry mum." Max informed her. "When we get back, we'll tell you all about it."

"Not so fast, what do you mean by 'You Four, you are going nowhere without supervision." Ellette told them.

"MUUUUM." Scarlet sounded disappointed.

They noticed that the crowd inside the restaurant were still watching them.

"We will discuss this more when we get home."

Four grumpy teenagers left to make their own way home, the journey home was not a happy one, the girls flew home with Scorzy, and the boys ran home with Lightning, leaving the four adults to make their own way home by car.

Confrontation

Surprise, surprise, the teenagers arrived some first, they were standing in a row across the front door with their arms folded, Scorzy was lying on the ground behind them, they looked very serious.

They adults walked through the garden gate then stood in a row across the garden path.

"I Think we are outnumbered." Justin stated.

Ellette whispered something and Snowball and Hairy Knees joined their number. "Now we are even."

"It's not a fight. It's supposed to be a discussion." Max informed them.

"Just being prepared." Mie laughed.

"Well, discuss your options." Jason said.

Max took a step forward.

"Mum's Dad's, well mums really, well Aunt Ellette actually you only found out about your powers at about the same age we are now, and then you were helped by Grandad Ling, we have had our powers and were able to use them from a very early age. Therefore, we are much more advanced than you were at our age and are much more capable of looking after ourselves. We will have Scorzy with us on the journey and we promise to return as soon as possible after he gets home. I'm sure you did not always do as you were asked, or told, when you were our age, if you knew that what you wanted to do was the correct thing, we have been talking to Gran and Grandad, do you want us to tell you what they told us, and Dads, we **know** you two got up to some mischief when you were younger, well?"

The four adults went on to a huddle.

"Just what are you doing?" Demanded Scarlet.

Mie looked up. "We are discussing our options." she responded.

After a few minutes, the adults seemed to be getting very animated. The teenagers heard the occasional whisper like, 'we could always' 'shush' 'but what if' 'why don't we' 'shush' 'are we all agreed?' then they were quite for a few seconds, then Justin was pushed out to face the teenagers.

"Eh, well" he acted and sounded a bit nervous. "We have, eh, reached a decision, we accept your decision to go on your adventure."

the teenagers jumped about in excitement. "But on condition that you, all of you go and inform your grandparents first thing tomorrow, and you tell us exactly where you are going, agreed?"

Then the four teenagers went into their own discussion huddle, complete with a lot of giggling. After a short time, Max came forward and stated. "We accept your terms."

Excited hugs all round.

Telling their grandparents was easier than expected, they took Scorzy with them, with an eight metre long Dragon to protect them, well, who could say no.

Expedition time

"Where are you going first?" Ellette asked. The four adults were there to give them a good send off.

The four adventurers, complete with back packs for goodies and essentials, stood before her.

"Lock Ness first of all, Scorzy says there is information there that can help us."

"That's only a couple of hours away, you could be back by teatime."

"MUUUM, we are going on an adventure, hopefully it will take longer than that." Scarlet told her.

"Have you packed cake." Scorzy asked.

"Yes, Scorzy, I mean Scorzist, I have packed some cake for you. You will take care now, won't you? And don't let too many people see you." it had been decided not to make Scorzist invisible. Ellette as well as Mie were getting a bit anxious, their brood had never been away from the family before, and she imagined all sorts of bad things happening to them.

"MUUUUM." Tilly was a bit tearful as well, so she went and gave her mum a big hug, they all followed her example. Ten minutes later with all hugs complete, the boys got on Scorzist back, waved goodbye, they jumped into the air, flew up over the roof tops and were off into the big unknown. For the four teenagers going off on their own was a big step to take, even if there was an eight metre long Dragon going with them.

Not being seen was a possible problem, they did not want to fly too low, to be seen by people on the ground, or too high, to be seen by people in aircraft. Max decided that seeing an eight metre long object fifteen hundred metres way would be difficult.

"Scorzy, if we fly at about fifteen hundred meters from the ground that would make it difficult for people to see us, and as the weather is not very good, and the sky is grey, can you change your colour to match that of the sky." Max asked.

"Why not want people to see us, would be great fun?" Scorzist commented.

"Do you want to be caught and put in a cage, because that could happen if the wrong people saw us." Max told him.

"No, not want that. Ok, me change." he adjusted his altitude and changed colour to a silvery grey.

"Hey, it looks as if there are two young boys floating along in the sky." Tilly said.

Scorzist turned his head towards her and smiled, showing off his shiny white teeth, they all laughed. They were leaving their border homeland behind and heading north towards the rolling hills of Ayrshire.

"We need to avoid the flight paths of the aircraft taking off and landing at Prestwick and Glasgow airports." Scarlet observed.

"So why don't we head further west and fly along the coast, and if anybody does see us, they might think we're seagulls." Tilly added.

"Good idea" Max told her. "But they are just Gulls, there are no such things as seagulls, all the sea birds are just members if the gull family."

"OOO! Who's been reading their encyclopaedia then." tilly chided.

"Who wants encyclopaedias when all the information is on the internet, so much easier." Max replied.

Gabriel had been paying attention to their surroundings.

"Small plane outbound from Prestwick, coming towards us." he told them.

"Who's for having a bit of fun then?" Tilly asked.

"Mum said, no silliness, remember." Scarlet scolded her.

"Spoil sport. What's life without a bit of fun, Boring." Tilly added.

Then they noticed that the small plane had suddenly changed direction and was now flying away from them.

"Ah well, next time." Tilly said a bit disgruntled.

A Few minutes later they were flying up the river Clyde estuary and could see the sun shining of the rippling water of Loch Lomond, and the highlands on the far distance.

"What a stunning view." Someone said.

"Yes, it is!" Relied Scarlet.

"What is?" Tilly asked.

"Someone said it was a stunning view, so I said 'yes, it is." Scarlet replied.

"Well, I never said it was a stunning view." Tilly said.

"Neither did I." "Or me" the boys said together.

The girls looked at each other, then nodded.

"OK Mum, show yourself; we know you are there." The girls said together.

Ellette, holding Mie, appeared flying beside them.

"MUUUM, do you not trust us." Ellette smiled. "Did you just make that small plane fly away from us?"

"Would I do a thing like that?" She said shyly.

"YES, you would." The boys added.

"We are doing fine, please go back home and let us do this ourselves." Scarlet pleaded.

"We just care about you so much that we wanted to be there just in case something went wrong." Mie explained.

"Mum, how are we going to grow up if we are not allowed to make some decisions on our own." Gabriel stated.

"Well?" Max added, arms folded in annoyance.

Ellette was a bit embarrassed at being caught so early.

"**IF**, we need help we will call for you, **OK?**"

"OK, just making sure you were all right, we'll go back home then, bye." she turned round and headed back the way they had come.

"Do you think they have gone back home?" the boys asked.

"How am I supposed to know? but we can always become invisible so they can't follow us." Scarlet said.

"We can't make ourselves invisible." Max said.

"But we can." then the girls vanished.

"Hey, that's not fair." Gabriel complained.

"SO, do you want to join us?" a bodyless voice said.

"YES" the boys shouted.

Then there was four invisible teenagers and a dragon flying towards the highlands at over one hundred kilometres per hour. They decided to drop lower and have some fun.

Saturday afternoon and the shopping centre at the south end of Loch Lomond was busy. One of the automatic things that happen when you are invisible, and flying, and having fun, is that you can't help but laugh.

They were flying at a very low level, about 10 metres. over the car park and shopping centre which was packed with people. The more people looked up to see who was laughing, the more they laughed. The more Scorzist laughed the harder they all laughed, if you had ever heard a Dragon laugh, then you would know why they were laughing so much.

"We need to land somewhere quickly, we've got a problem." Tilly said anxiously.

"Problem, what Problem?" the other three asked in alarm,

"I need to go to the loo." Tilly giggled.

"Me too." Laughed Scorzist, they laughed even harder.

They circled the large car park a few times to give themselves time to calm down, they found a quiet corner furthest away from the shops and glided down then landed. They were still invisible, but some people were looking over in their direction.

"What do we do now, do we go to the loo invisible? That could prove to be tricky." "Gabriel said.

"It's ok for you boys, you could just use the nearest bush, and nobody would know." Tilly scolded.

A large wet patch appeared on the carpark.

"Oops, too late." Scorzist said through his invisible smile.

Some people looked over at the area where they were because they all burst out laughing again.

"I need to go now?" tilly exclaimed.

"We can go to the toilets invisible, become visible in tie toilet then walk back as normal." Scarlet stated.

"Ok. Let's go. Now." Tilly said.

After a few seconds Max said. "Are you away yet?" he listened then added. "Must be. this just is so weird. I Know let's pretend we are not here when they get back."

A Few minutes later the girls returned, they had thought something like this would happen.

"Oh, this is terrible we can't find the boys." Tilly exclaimed.

"Ready?" Scarlet whispered. Tilly nodded. Scarlet snapped her fingers. and the two boy's heads appeared. Only their heads.

The boys screamed, and the girls laughed.

Scorzist roared "GREAT FUN."

Now that did draw attention to them, and a number of people started to come over to see what was happening.

Scarlet snapped her fingers and the boy's heads disappeared.

"Are you alright, we heard somebody scream?" Someone asked.

"Eh, no we're fine I just twisted my ankle." Tilly lied.

"Are you sure, are your parents about?" Another person asked.

"We're fine we're just having a day out." Scarlet answered.

A girl of about ten peeked out from behind her mum.

"I know who you are, you're Tilly and Scarlet Queen Ellette's daughters. I've seen your pictures in magazines do you really have wings like your mum?"

They could hardly be mistaken for anybody else, after all they were celebrities, as they were growing up, everywhere they went they had their photograph taken. They had sharp elven feature, long silvery white hair, and bright shining eyes, just like their mum, the whole world knew about and recognised Queen Ellette after she became the leader of all Magical creatures a number of years earlier.

"Yes, we have wings" Scarlet said, feeling quite embarrassed.

"Can I see them, please?" the girl askes politely.

The took off their jackets and unfurled their wings, the crown gasped, a lot of people still did not believe in that Fairy story.

"They got to be fake." A middle age man called as he moved towards them. Then it looked as if he had walked into a brick wall. His arms were pinned to his side, and he could not move.

The crowd heard a soft but deep giggle, then the voice said 'Cake.'

The girl was holding a large muffin in her hand.

"OH, OH, now we have got a problem." a young male voice stated.

The crowd backed away.

"Let him go Scorzy." Scarlet said in a whisper, but it was still loud enough for the crowd to hear.

"What was that?" the man said as he stumbled backwards.

"We are on a rescue mission; we are trying to get one of our friends back to his own people." Tilly told them.

"What kind of friend can do that?" The man queried.

"A Dragon friend." the girl said, "a big silvery blue Dragon friend." then she whispered. "I believe in Fairies."

"Aw, can I have your cake, me like cake." a deep voice said.

Everyone, except the little girl stepped back even further.

"Might as well then, Golden Scorzy?" Scarlet asked

"OK." the deep voice called.

Scarlet snapped her fingers, the two boys as well as a golden Dragon appeared.

"HI." they said, then waved at the frightened crowd, well they were all frightened except the little girl who held out her muffin to Scorzist, he accepted it gently, then swallowed it whole.

"Thank you, that was really kind of you."

The girls mum ran forward and pulled her back out of the way.

"Careful he doesn't eat you." she said anxiously.

"Aw, Not eat people, don't breathe fire, like cake." Scorzist said then giggled.

"I just knew Dragons were real" The little girl said excitedly as she ran forward to give him a hug. The crowd gasped.

"I think we should leave now and get on with our journey, we still have a long way to go." Max again came up with the solution to their immediate problem.

Max and Gabriel climbed on to Scorzy's back and he gracefully took to the skies, Tilly and Scarlet flapped their wings and rose gently into the air, more people could see them now, they thought they should make the best of the situation, so they looped round the car park and over the shopping area. So many people waved and cheered as they flew out over the loch, scaring a few people who out on their boats, they flew up the Loch and out of site.

Tilly and Scarlet were flying beside Scorzist, one on either side. Tilly looked across at Scarlet and smiled, Scarlet looked back as if to say, 'what are you up to now?'

"Scorzy, do you like fish?"

"Apart from being wet and slimy, yes do. Why?"

"There must be a lot of fish down there" she nodded down towards the water.

"OOO." Scorzist said excitedly, before starting to dive towards the loch.

"NO, Scorzy NOOO." the boys shouted, the girls stated to laugh.

Scorzist dived into the water then swam or was he flying just under the surface with the boys surfing on his back. After the initial shock they were laughing so hard. They were approaching the narrow channel of water between the islands of Inchmoan. and Inchcruin, where they saw what seemed like a sparkly cloud fluttering near the shore, then the cloud seemed to move across the water towards them.

Scorzist and the two girls stopped.

"It's Fairies, it's a Frollick of Fairies." Tilly shouted excitedly "They're coming out to see us." she would have jumped up and down if she could have, but it's difficult to jump when you're flying.

The Frollick of Fairies flew out to meet them, about one hundred in all, they were flying around them making their high pitched tinkling noise which sounded like a very small fine silver stars falling on to a silver tray, some of them landed on the girls shoulders.

"They are dancing because they are so happy to see us, and they so happy that Queen Ellette has set the Magical kingdom free, they also say they are not Fairies as we know; they are called Dryads and they live in the Willow trees along the shores of the loch." Tilly said, she noticed that the boys looked a little dejected.

"What's wrong with you two?" Scarlet asked them.

"You two are, you can talk to Fairies, and do magic, and fly, and become invisible, we are useless, we feel we are just along for the ride."

Tilly spoke to the Dryads, and they flew off south.

"What did you say to them?" Max asked.

"I told them there was a little girl down at the end of the loch who would love to see them."

"So, what do we do now?" Gabriel asked.

"How fast can you run?" Scarlet asked the boys.

"We are not quite sure." Max Answered.

"How about finding out then." she asked with a cheeky smile.

"What do you mean, there is only water all around us?" Max observed.

Scarlet pointed up the loch.

"That island up there in front of us is called Inchlonaig and the near one on the left is called Inchconnachan, pick one and we will race to it, that is if you are up for a challenge?" Scarlet challenged.

"On the water, we have to run on the water?" Gabriel looked shocked.

"If you can?" she added.

The boys looked at each other, then nodded.

"Ok, GO." the boys shouted suddenly, then ran as fast as they could towards the nearer island.

At first, they started to sink, then they ran faster and gained confidence, soon they found that they could actually run across the surface of the loch. The faster they ran the harder they laughed.

"Time to go." Tilly told Scarlet. They flew after the boys, who were very fast, but flying was faster, and soon the girls overtook the boys, they were all laughing so hard they did not notice Scorzist passing them overhead. When they got to the island Scorzist was waiting for them.

"Me win." Scorzist told them smugly. "Does the winner get cake?"

Tilly took some cake out of her bag and gave it to Him.

Scorzist smiled. "Happy Dragon." he said.

"Happier now?" Scarlet asked the boys "We have got to do things, so that we can find what we are good at."

After a short rest, and more cake, they were off again on what they hoped would be the final part of their journey. They reached the end of the loch and were soon flying over some of the most stunning scenery in the world, the Scottish Highlands. High craggy peaks, with Ben Nevis furthest away, the sun glinting off the granite rocks, so many lochs and rivers shining like silver in the sunshine, even patches of snow where the sun never reached, purple heather and so many trees, in so many different shades of green it was difficult to count.

"Hey, we missed lunch, and I'm hungry, where can stop for something to eat, **and** we need to find somewhere to stay tonight, **and** I'm sure we won't be able to book into a hotel" Max as always was the pragmatic voice of reason.

"Place to stay, Scorzist knows places to stay." he told the youngsters.

"Ok, burger bar with shopping centre nearby, Inverness is the place to go, OK?"

"Well actually Fort William is nearer, then we can go to Loch Ness tomorrow." Max informed them.

"YES, Fort William is good." Scorzist added. "Find good place to stay near Fort William.

They were flying invisible again and landed in a car park on the edge of town.

"Scorzy, can we trust you to stay here, and stay hidden until we get back?" Scarlet asked, he was about to say something "and yes, we will bring you some cake." Scarlet said, Scorzist smiled and nodded his head before becoming invisible again.

Burger bar, no chance, Fish and Chips was what they decided on, which they ate as they wandered about the town centre, then into a local supermarket to get cake. They did not realise that cake, especially the amount they were going to buy, was so going to be so expensive.

"We don't have enough money to buy enough cake?" Gabriel stated.

"I've been thinking about that." Tilly said. "We left in such a hurry, we forgot to bring extra money with us."

"I have a solution." Scarlet told them. They looked at her with concern.

"MUUUM, we need some more money." she held out her hand. A collection of bank notes appeared in her hand. "Thanks mum."

"Isn't magic just so wonderful" Scarlet smiled.

"Has she been with as all this time." Max asked.

"Not Physically, in spirt only, she has had other Magical creatures looking after us." A small wood sprite appeared beside them, smiled then vanished. "Did you think that our parents would let the four of us out of their sight without finding a way to keep an eye on us."

"I suppose they just want to know we're safe." Gabriel added.

"Come on, time we were getting back to our tame Dragon."

Back at the carpark, there was no sign of Scorzist, well there wouldn't be because he was invisible, but they knew he would want to get his cake as soon as they returned. They heard a winged beating noise approaching, which grew in strength.

"Scorzy, where have you been?" Tilly asked as she felt Scorzist landing next to them>

"Went to see them, make sure we have place to stay tonight."

"Them, who is them?" Max Asked.

"Cake first then find out, keep some cake for them, they like cake."

Scorzist had a good helping of cake, but he made sure there was plenty left over for a second meal, with them.

They lifted off from the car park and headed out over the vast expanse of trees which stretched in front of them. Scorzist was leading them far into the forest. Light was fading, the sun was setting behind the mountains.

"What are you looking for Scorzy?" Tilly asked.

"That down there." in the distance they saw a small clearing, which seemed to be glowing in the darkening forest, he headed down towards it. He dropped down through the trees and landed in the clearing. The tees seemed to close over them like a canopy. The girls landed beside him.

They heard a soft murmur coming from the trees, then a whole colony of wood elves came dancing from behind the trees and danced around them, such a joyful thing to behold.

"Have cake." Scorzist told them, he then laid the cake on the ground.

The high Elf of the colony walked over, stopped in front of them. then bowed.

"We are honoured to have such special guests visit our humble Colony." his voice sounded so musical.

Tilly noticed the boys looked puzzled, she realised they were speaking in Elvish, and the boys could not understand what was being said.

"I give you the gift of Elven speech." the boys eyes lit up in excitement.

"And we are grateful for this gift of cake. This is such a special occasion for us to have our Queen Ellette's daughters and Mie's sons staying with us."

"We are most grateful for your hospitality." Tilly and Scarlet said together, both then bowed.

"We just need some place to rest before continuing with our quest in the morning." Scarlet added.

"We have already prepared entertainment and refreshment for you, if you so wish?" the High Elf told them.

"That sounds like a great way to end our day." Gabriel found his voice after the initial surprise. "This is the first time we have visited an Elf colony; we would be delighted to join in with your festivities."

The Elves lived simple lives, their idea of entertainment and refreshment would never be accepted as a party in human society. They played simple instrument made out of wood, mainly whistles and drums, but their singing was so serene and soothing, and ever so relaxing. Their refreshments were clear spring water and fruits of the forest served with bread or biscuits, simple and wholesome.

"This is how the whole world should live, no pressure and no stress, just so relaxing." Gabriel told the others.

"Do you think you could live like this all the time. For the rest of your life, or do you think you would miss your computer games?" Tilly asked him.

"Well, I suppose weekends like this would make a real difference to peoples' lives, but all the time? probably not." He responded.

Sitting on the soft fragrant grass they were so relaxed, before they knew what was happening, they were all sound asleep, well it had been a busy day. They were awakened in the morning to the sound of birds singing, breakfast was already waiting for them, more spring water, served with biscuits, fresh fruit, and honey.

When you are in a happy place it is often difficult to leave, but leave they had to, their quest was not yet fulfilled.

With full stomachs and spirts as high as they could be, they said goodbye to their elven friends then flew out of the clearing and up into the early morning sunshine. The sun was shining across the forest creating a multi coloured patchwork in the treetops, with the three lochs stretching out in front of them shining like a silver ribbon glinting in the morning sunshine. Loch Ness, the one furthest away beckoned them towards their final goal.

"Scorzy, do you know where you are going?" Max asked.

"I think so, been a long time." Scorzist replied.

"You don't sound very confident." Gabriel commented.

Scorzist seemed very unhappy.

"Scorzy, are you trying to tell us something?" Scarlet asked.

"Well." Scorzist said shyly.

"Scorzy, out with it, tell us what you are thinking." Max demanded.

"Don't know if really want to go home. Fun being here, and with you guys, and the Fairies, and the Elves."

"Do you mean being HERE, or with us? because we can't be here all the time, we will need to go home." Scarlet asked.

"BOTH, or all four."

"**Scorzy**" shouted Tilly angrily. "You mean we have come all the way here for **nothing**?"

"NO, NO, NO, not nothing, show you something really, what you say, REALLY COOL"

"Something really cool?" asked Max sceptically.

"Something really, really cool, but need to wait till there is darkness."

"Could you not have shown us the cool thing last night?" Gabriel asked.

"Not in proper place last night, will be tonight." Scorzist told them with a smile.

"So, what are we going to do for the rest of the day?" Max asked.

"Have fun." Scorzist told them as he flew down to the surface of the loch.

Even splashing about in Loch Ness has its limitations, after a few hours, they were getting bored.

The elves had given them food for lunch before they left, bread, biscuits, fruit, and honey.

"Let's go and sit on the shore and have our lunch." they were still invisible. "We should find a place where there is nobody about. it would be better if we were able to see each other." Max decided.

They found a quite shaded area to sit, where Scorzist could stay under the trees, just in case somebody passed by on the loch.

"This why like this place, what you say? is beautiful, yes?"

"OH yes, such a beautiful place." Tilly agreed.

Lazy day, warm sunshine, lying back on the soft grass, so easy to fall asleep, which they all did.

Someone shouting 'HELP, HELP, HELP' will always wake you up if you are dozing and that's just what happened.

"Who's shouting for help?" Max was the first awake.

"Help my dad's not well." a voice called from far out on the loch.

Scarlet flew up through the trees to get a better view of the loch.

"There is a boy with a two-man canoe away out on the loch, but I can only see one person." before she was finished the boys were running out towards the boy with the canoe. Tilly joined Scarlet and they both flew after the boys.

Max and Gabriel got there first, and the girls were not far behind.

"My dad" the young lad said. "he said he didn't feel well then he fell out of the canoe, help him please, I don't know where he is, he must be under the water."

The four teenagers felt so frustrated there was nothing they could do, suddenly the water beside the canoe sort of exploded and a dark green Scorzist Mogg appeared with the young lad's dad on his back.

"Well done Scorzy, quickly get him to the other shore I can see a car over there, girls fly over and get them to call for an ambulance, quickly" Max ordered "We'll bring the young lad and the canoe."

The lady on the shore got a fright when her son started calling for help for his dad, she got an even greater shock when she saw two boys running across the loch, then two girls flying as well, then the huge green monster rising up out of the water with her husband on its back. She didn't faint, well not quite, but it took her a few seconds to understand what was happening.

"Call for an ambulance." one of the flying girls shouted to her, which she did right away.

The girls knew all about the time when their mum flew the injured girl to the hospital, but this man was too heavy to carry, even with both of them working together.

The woman froze as Scorzist crawled out of the water, the girls helped get the man off his back and onto the grassy shore. The woman was just gazing at Scorzist, 'Boo' he said quietly. She jumped back, then focused on her husband.

"I'm a nurse, what happened out there?"

"He sounded as though he was choking then he fell into the water, I shouted for help, then *they* turned up to help." her son told her.

She quickly examined her husband; he was breathing, and his heart was beating strongly.

"He's unconscious but seems stable for now; we will just need to make him comfortable and wait till the ambulance arrives. Who are you four and are you Nessie?" she asked.

"That's Queen Ellette's daughters and Mie's sons." the boy told his mum.

"Are you really Nessie?" Scorzist just smiled.

"It seems we are more famous than we thought, is there nowhere we can go where we will not be recognised?" Scarlet stated.

"Scorzy, are you bigger than you used to be?" Max asked.

"Magic food, magic water, Scorzy grows." he laughed.

"You better get out of here before the ambulance arrives." Tilly told him. He slid back towards the loch and was soon submerged.

"He, it, the, Nessie the monster, it can talk?" the woman stuttered.

"He's not a monster, he's a Dragon, please don't tell anybody you have seen him, it would take quite a lot of explaining." Gabriel said. They could hear sirens in the distance and they were approaching very fast.

Now he knew that his dad was safe, the boy who as about fourteen years old was now staring at the girls.

"Wow, nobody's at school is going to believe this actually happened, can I get a selfie with you?"

"The joy of being a celebrity." Scarlet whispered then added. "as long as you don't mention Nessie, Deal?"

"Wow, deal." he said excitedly, his sick dad totally forgotten.

The photo was taken just a s the ambulance arrived. The crew got out, then froze when they saw who was there.

"Come on then your patient is over here." Gabriel beckoned them.

They checked the man over but could find no real problems, it was decided that they should get him to hospital a soon as possible, he was loaded into the ambulance which took off with blue lights flashing and sirens sounding.

"What can I do to thank you for saving my husband's life." the woman asked.

"Nothing, we are just glad we were in the right place at the right time, and that we had Scorzy with us." Max told her.

"Scorzy?" she asked.

"Scorzist Mogg, that's his name, we are helping him to get home, at least we thought we were, but it seems that he likes it here and wants to stay." Max told her.

"I would be such a life saver if he could, I must get to the hospital now, goodbye." The woman and her son got into the car and left.

"Hey, I have just had a great idea." Gabriel said with a grin.

"Oh, Oh, I don't like it when Gabriel has an idea." Tilly commented.

"Let's go find Scorzy first." Gabriel said keeping them in suspense. They made their way back to the other side of the loch, Scorzist was there waiting for them.

"Scorzy, you are huge, you must be over ten metres long now."

"Nessie size again." Scorzist laughed.

"Come on then what's the great idea?" Scarlet asked.

"Scorzy could stay here and just be Nessie." Gabriel said.

"You know you do have some weird ideas." Till told him.

"What's so weird about it, so many people come here to try and catch a glimpse of Nessie, well let them, Scorzy could show himself sometimes, and that would bring in more tourists, I don't mean he would fly up and down the loch shouting here I am, he could just pop up to the surface sometimes or swim just underneath the surface, just to keep people interested, well?" Gabriel paused.

"And feed Scorzy cake, Scorzy like that." he smiled.

"People don't know you eat cake Scorzy." Max told him.

"How will Scorzy get cake?" he asked.

"I have an idea about that as well." Gabriel stated. "Let me make a phone call. He pulled out his mobile phone logged on to the internet then dialled a number.

"Can I speak to the manager please." the other three could only hear Gabriel's side of the conversation.

"Thank you."

"Is that the Manager?"

"My name? My name is max, have you heard of Tilly, Scarlet, Gabriel, and Maximillian."

Long pause.

"Yes, good, well I am Maximillian, and I, well we have a proposition for you, we would like to meet you somewhere."

"Yes, it would benefit you."

"Where? Urquhart Castle in one hour, and make sure the castle is closed to the public, we don't want anybody else to be there."

"Thank you, oh, and by the way can you bring some cake please."

"Yes, I said cake, lots of cake, and it's not for us, it's for a special visitor."

"Thank you, see you in one hour."

"What was all that about." Scarlet asked.

"That was the Manager of the Loch Ness centre at Drumnadrochit. We are going to introduce him to Nessie." Gabriel told them.

"What!" they all said together. "Why?"

"Scorzy wants a home, why not here, we can even get him cake whenever he wants it."

They planned how best to introduce Nessie to his new employer. An hour later the four teenagers were standing in the grounds of the castle, a man dressed in a smart suit approached them, he was holding a carrier bag that seemed to be quite heavy. Max walked up to him.

"Good afternoon, I am Max, would you like to meet Nessie?" he asked the man.

"If this is a joke it's not very funny." The man said to Max.

"Oh, it's not a joke. and the cake is for him." Max replied.

"I always thought that Nessie was female?"

"Things are not always what they seem, Yes or No?" Max asked.

"Ok go on show me your trick." The man did not look very happy at all. Max smiled, raised his arm and waved. They were standing as high up on the castle as they could get.

Scorzist had been flying about invisible, the waving hand was his signal to dive into the water, there was loud splash, and they could see a disturbance in the water about two hundred metres away.

After a short time, they could see something dark under the surface of the loch, it was moving towards them. As it got closer it got bigger and bigger, suddenly Scorzist pushed his head above the surface then walked up the back towards them. The man nearly fainted.

"Hello." Scorzist rumbled. The man tried to step back, tripped and fell onto his backside.

"Do males have to fall on their backside every time they get a shock." Tilly and Scarlet laughed.

"Mr manager I would like you to meet our friend Scorzist Mogg. He is looking for somewhere to make his home, and he likes it here."

"Scorzist likes cake, you got cake for Scorzist?"

The Manager held up the bag he as carrying.

"I couldn't get a lot of cake, so I brought along doughnuts as well." He stammered.

"What is doughnuts?" Scorzist asked.

"Doughnuts are really nice Scorzy." Scarlet told him, she took one out of the bag and held out up for him to sniff.

"Smell Ok, me try doughnuts." Scarlet through the doughnut into the air, Scorzist caught it in his mouth.

"Nice, like doughnuts, want more."

"Mr Manager, how would you like Scorzist to be the new attraction in Loch Ness." Max Asked the man.

"Nothing can replace Nessie." He said.

"Scorzist is, or was Nessie, he has been around for over ten thousand years, we believe he was the original Nessie. You could arrange for someone to take a photograph of him swimming in the loch and call him Dragon Nessie, just think of the publicity and all the people that would come here to see him, and all you would need to do is feed him cake."

"People might try to catch him." he added.

"We will leave Scorzy with a Fairy gift; he will be able to make himself invisible whenever he wants to." Tilly Said smiling.

"Scorzy, go fly under the water please." Tilly asked.

Scorzist jumped into the water and swam just under the surface.

"Wow, now that is impressive." the man stated. "we could arrange tours on the water and guarantee that the punters could catch sight of him without getting too close, I think we have a deal." He turned round and shook Max's hand.

"Scorzist, are you happy to stay nearby?"

"Scorzist say yes, Scorzist has friends nearby."

"What friends Scorzy?" Tilly asked.

"Find out later, more doughnuts first, happy Scorzist" then he smiled. "We have more journey to do first. We be back later Mr Manager."

Max took the bag of cakes and doughnuts from the Manager then they took off and flew towards Inverness.

"Scorzist, why are we going to Inverness?" Gabriel asked.

"Feeding time, then we go hunting for magical things."

"I know this will be a silly question, but what magical things." Gabriel asked.

"Find out later, need to wait till dark." Scorzist told them.

"You do like your fun Scorzy." Max commented.

"HEE, HEE, Yes, maybe should say AYE," Scorzist rumbled.

The landed near Inverness, the four youngsters went to get a carry out, as well as more cake for the always hungry Scorzist.

As the sun was going down and the light was fading, they made their way west.

"We go first to Reelig Glen, where big trees are, magic make trees grow big." Scorzist informed them. They landed in a beautiful glen just before the sun set.

"Look at the size of those trees." Tilly said excitedly.

"Need unicorn horn to look for magic things."

Scarlet had been trusted with the Unicorn horn that Lightning had brought them. She took it out of her bag.

"We look for tracks in the dark." Scorzist told them.

They walked along the path. Scarlet was holding the Unicorn horn in front of her. The horn was shining but not very brightly, there was some small sparkly shapes on the path.

"Not magic here. They been here but not here tonight, need to go another place." Scorzist said.

They flew further west towards Glen Affric, which is supposed to be the most beautiful glen in Scotland.

"I feel something, there is a tingling, it feels as if the air is full of magic." Scarlet told them as they landed.

"I Feel it too." Tilly said.

"Must be great to be a Magical Fairy." Gabriel complained.

"We all have our part to play, it took **all of us** to save that man earlier today, yes?" Scarlet chided him.

"Ok, I get it, sorry." he said shyly.

Scarlet brought out the Unicorn horn and started to walk along the path, right away the horn was shining so much brighter, and it was showing up sparkly marks on the path.

"They are here." Scorzist told them.

"Who are **they.**" Scarlet asked.

"They helped me, follow marks and see." he told them.

As they walked along the marks got clearer.

"They look like small hoof prints, are they ponies?" Tilly asked.

"Not ponies, follow, not far now." Scorzist told them.

The main path went ahead, but the hoof prints followed a narrower path into the trees then stopped at a tall smooth rock face.

"They here, look for small round hole in rocks."

Scarlet used the light from the horn and soon found a small perfectly round hole hidden in one of the cracks in the rock face.

"Put horn in hole." Scorzist told scarlet. She pushed the horn into the hole. It was a perfect fit. Silence was all around them, there had been nighttime animal noises before, but now there was only silence. The rock face started to shimmer and grow lighter, as if there was a light shining through it from the other side. Colours started to show in the rock, every colour you could think of was now shining on them. They saw something moving in the light and it was coming towards them.

"It's a Unicorn, no, it's lots of Unicorns." Scarlet screamed excitedly then turned to Scorzist. "is this Unicorn land?"

Scorzist nodded.

"Wow, it's like all the rainbows in the world are shining at the same time, and all in the same place. There are hundreds of unicorns, and they are all different colours as well, it's just so beautiful." Scarlett was just so stunned.

A pale purple unicorn. Lilac really, stopped in front them and bowed it's head. The four teenagers returned the bow. The Unicorn backed away as if to say. 'Please enter out home.'

As they entered, the rock wall behind them returned to being just a rock wall.

"They are just ponies. There are none as big as lightning." Gabriel stated.

It was as if the Unicorn with them understood what they said, but the Unicorn could not speak but it put a thought in each of their minds.

"Lightning is not a real Unicorn, he was created by Queen Ellette's imagination and by the power from her mind, as is her other helpers, we are living Unicorns, hidden here since the beginning of time, where we live in peace, but sometimes contact others of the Magical community, we knew you were searching for us that is why we gave the Unicorn horn to Lightning."

"We are grateful for your gift we will keep your home a secret." Tilly told them.

"Thank you, Princess Tilly."

"What did you just call me?"

"You are the daughters of Queen Ellette therefore you are Princess Tilly, and Princess Scarlet. The sons of Mei, Queen Ellette's assistant, are Prince Maximillian and Prince Gabriel.

"Wow, never thought of myself as a Prince, sounds good though, Prince Gabriel."

"Now who's getting big headed." Scarlet chided.

"Yes, your Majesty." Gabriel replied with a laugh.

"Seen so many Kings, Queens, Princes and princesses, ten thousand years long time to wander, Scorzist feel he is home."

They all laughed. They were made so welcome and looked after so well that they stayed until the next morning.

They promised that they would visit the Unicorns again, and that Queen Ellette would also visit them. They left the beautiful Glen

Affric behind them. It was even more stunning in the morning sunshine and headed towards loch ness.

Scorzist was quite emotional as they sat on the banks of Loch ness, getting ready to fly home.

"Hey, we can't fly, how are we going to get home?" Max said.

"Do you think we should give the boys wings?" Scarlet asked Tilly.

"**No.**" Max Screamed. "We don't want wings. It's only a few hundred miles we can run home." He told the girls.

"No need, we have arranged for you to get a ride home, Lightning." Scarlet called, and lightning appeared in all his magical glory.

"Is this going to be a race then." The boys climbed onto the back of Lightning who reared up and took off as fast as only lightning can.

The girls said their goodbyes to Scorzist and again promised that they would return to see him.

The boys were a long way ahead.

"When will these boys ever grow up, yes?" Tilly asked Scarlet.

"OH! yes, the race is on." Scarlet replied as they took off as fast as they could.

"You know Tilly this tale is going to take some telling when we get home. Just who is going to believe that we spent the night in Unicorn land. Faster Tilly **faster.**

The end. Absolutely?

PART 8

Scorzist Mogg - A Short Dragons Tale

It really is an unusual sensation when you open your eyes for the first time and discover that you are a baby Dragon, awesome. Not only that, but you are a Golden baby Dragon, must be so special to be golden, then parents go and name you Scorzist, just what kind of name is that, but hey, being a Dragon, just how cool is that. then you realise that everyone else is a Dragon as well, kinda takes that fun out of it, but hey ho, could be worse, could have been born human, now that would be scary.

One of the best things about being a baby Dragon is that when you come out of your egg on day one, just like a baby crocodile, you don't need anyone to look after you, freedom comes as standard, and happily there were no bad things in our Dragon world to hunt you. Perhaps that was problem, there was nobody to tell Scorzist what not to do, so if wanted to do something, just did it. Scorzist not a bad Dragon just a bit mischievous, well more than a bit, in fact quite a lot, always getting told off for doing things that Scorzist thought were, well, just fun. Like hiding when parents were looking for me and hiding again when it was time to go to the learning place, and what's wrong with jumping on adult's backs to get a free lift somewhere, they are going there anyway. Or my favourite pastime, eating cake, especially other people's cake, Scorzist likes cake, eat other things as well but cake is the best ever. No, that wrong, cake was much later in new world, there was no cake in dragon land, so sad.

Dragon land was so big and so nice, caves to hide in, big tall trees and cliffs to climb and jump off to test wings, baby Dragons need time to build up strength in wings, deep rivers and lakes to swim in, lots of nice Dragon things to eat, but no cake.

Scorzist used to jump off big high cliffs with wings folded till just before hitting ground, then use wings to fly away, other Dragons used to laugh at Scorzist, but Scorzist didn't care about others that were scared to follow Scorzist in his challenges. Often called stupid and weird but not care, just liked being Scorzist.

After years of naughtiness other Dragons got so annoyed with Scorzist that they started to say to other Dragons that were naughty, you are a just being a SCORZIST. Me famous, Ha Ha.

Dragon land is so safe Scorzist was running out of challenges, what to do? me know, leave Dragon land, and see what other challenges life has.

Scorzist still young and small, only about one hundred years old and as long as would wrap round middle-sized tree.

Rules, always rules, Scorzist not like rules, always did opposite of what told not to do, that was how found way out of Dragon land. Don't go to deep in the lake, was told, went deep anyway, got colder, went deeper, and colder, and darker, no light, kept going through small narrow tunnel, saw light, swam towards light, found way to big dark water in new land, found out later big dark water called Loch Ness.

New land was so cold, and food was different, found fish to eat, fish ok, found berries and eggs, not eat birds because birds law eggs, no birds no eggs. Flew high up to clouds, big place, lots of cold ice, need to find place to call home. Saw funny things moving about on ground, had to find out what they were, had four legs like Scorzist, fluffy tail not like Scorzist, longer legs that Scorzist and pointy thing sticking out of forehead, looked so funny. Flew down to see them, they so much taller than Scorzist, and have funny feet, not claws like Scorzist, never seen anything like them before, but they friendly, they gather round and tell me they are called Unicorns, they not speak Dragon but put words in Scorzist's head so that he understands. They take Scorzist home to their magic place, beautiful place, have lots of fun, give food and keep Scorzist warm. Magic food and place make Scorzist grow, told live there for hundreds of years, time to leave and find new places to go in big new world. Unicorns show Scorzist how to get back to their magic land, if he wishes.

Not so much ice or snow now, unicorns tell there are people in new world that will not like

Scorzist, they not like things that are different, should stay away from them, but Scorzist need to find out for himself. Scorzist fly everywhere, see more people, some see Scorzist and chase him away, they not like Dragons. Fly for many days over big water, see new people of different colours, different plants and different food. Some people happy to see Scorzist especially small noisy people, have fun with them, then big people chase Scorzist away, Scorzist not like big people. See big cold mountains with lots of snow, and deep valleys with lots of water, and places with lots of sand, no food there for Scorzist, so go back to place with big dark water and Unicorns. Magic place with Magic water, Scorzist grow big, learn to change colour so can hide easily, some people see Scorzist and call him monster. Visit many places, in new world, after long time meet with nice people called Elves, they Magical as well, they also tell Scorzist he should hide. So Scorzist hides, not eat much so shrinks to small size, so easier to hide, but still has to go find food. Visit small village and smell nice smell, go find out what smell is, find house, smell coming from inside house, window open, nice smell so tempting, so go inside house, hairy animal inside house, smaller than Unicorn and not have Horn. Scorzist eat thing of nice smell. People come, Scorzist leaves, hear people get angry they say 'Stupid dog, did you eat the cake?' Scorzist found cake, need to find mare places to get cake.

Hiding not good enough, Scorzist found by big silver Unicorn, then Queen Ellette and Mei come to get Scorzist and take him home. Happy Scorzist, but not big enough to talk to nice people. Until big birthday party and huge cake which Scorzist eats and grows so can talk, meets lots of nice people has lots of adventures and fun. Mei and Ellette say Dragons come from people's dreams, that just another fairy tale, no, not fairy tale, people tale.

Now Scorzist lives in big dark place called Loch Ness and given cake to stay there. People try to see Scorzist, Scorzist call this play time, some people try to catch Scorzist, have great fun annoying them.

'After more than ten thousand years Scorzist is home. Scorzist so happy now'.

The End, Absolutely this time